CHARLIE SIERRA TANGO

by

KENDALL GRACE

Dedication

To my very own pilot, who touched down safely on Walker's Cay every single flight. And to the island of Walker's. May someone restore you to your former glory so that we may visit you once again. You are sorely missed. Last but not least, I need to thank my wonderful editor, Kelli Collins, for making me a better writer.

CHAPTER ONE

"This will be our last time together."

Lawson Manning ran his hand lovingly along her smooth lines as he completed the last of his flight check. The Cessna 210 gleamed in the early-afternoon sun. She was still shiny and new, with less than a thousand hours on her. But she wasn't his.

Not that he was complaining. He'd scrimped and saved for three years to buy his baby, his escape from this hellhole job and its asshole boss.

Diego Charters had once been a blessing for a man whose aspirations of becoming a fighter pilot had been shattered by a damn eye exam—and the discovery that his particular issue couldn't be corrected with surgery. Amazing how much power the letter S could have when it was mistakenly identified as a Z. And not being able to see targets clearly was a problem for the United States Marine Corps, but not so much for shuttling clients to and from business meetings and to their sunny Florida and

Caribbean vacations.

But what had been a hell of a Plan B screeched to a halt when John Diego senior passed away suddenly from a heart attack and his dickwad son took the helm. John junior expected his employees to jump at the word go, probably from lack of any other sort of management skill. And they did. Lawson included, until he'd saved enough to buy his Piper Cherokee 6 and get the fuck out of there. He was nearly thirty. Not too late for his life to really get started.

He'd agreed to this last charter because John was in a bind. And if the truth be told, he wanted one last ride with the lady. He'd flown her maiden trip, after all, and he wasn't one to leave a ladybird without a proper goodbye. Lawson smirked. He'd stuck it to the man too, demanding twice his normal pay to take this charter to Treasure Cay.

Lawson was just putting the stepladder he'd used to check the fuel into the cargo hold when he heard a vehicle pull onto the tarmac. He closed the door, engaged the lock and turned. A limo. He heaved a weighted sigh.

Just one more and then I run my own show.

The driver opened the rear passenger door and one long, tanned leg followed by the other unfolded from the interior. His gaze traveled up in appreciation as his client emerged from the vehicle. Her mahogany hair whipped across her face in the wind and she slid her sunglasses atop her head, pinning the hair back.

Lawson sucked in a breath.

"Oh hell to the no."

Merilee Diego's vision was perfect, and she could see Lawson's scowl from thirty yards away. He could frown all he wanted. She wasn't happy about this trip either. But from the look on his face, clearly her brother had failed to mention she'd be Lawson's last charter. That was *so* a John thing to do. She was convinced he had the devil in him—fucking around with people for his own asinine amusement. Her fingers tightened around the leather handles of her bag. She jumped when the limo's trunk slammed, and turned to face the driver.

"Shall I take this to the plane for you, Miss Diego?"

"Yes, Charles. Thank you."

He gave her a nod and a smile and rolled her Louis Vuitton toward the Cessna. She reluctantly followed, second-guessing herself. Perhaps there was another way to gain the information she needed besides putting herself at the mercy of a man who clearly didn't care for her. What in the hell she'd done to him, she had no idea, but it was what it was. She shook her head.

Lawson Manning was the only person she could turn to.

She watched as he crossed his arms over his chest and planted his feet in a defensive stance. *Fantastic.*

She trailed behind Charles, feeling the heat of

Lawson's glare intensify the closer she got. He'd given her looks of distaste before, but not like the one he was laying on her now. If her father hadn't thought so highly of him, she would have likened him to an animal and been done with it. But Daddy seemed to have loved him like a son, and his name had been spoken of reverently in their home. *Lawson did this. Lawson said that.* It irked the hell out of her brother. If she were a betting woman, she'd go all in that her father had secretly wished his own son were more like Lawson.

She rolled her eyes. Her brother was an ass, but at least he didn't look at her like a piece of gum he'd just stepped in. When she got within spitting distance of Lawson and the ice-blue of his gaze pierced her, she began to regret her plan. It was too late now though.

"Merilee," he drawled in that thick South Georgia accent she'd deny to her grave that she loved. Even laced with irritation it sounded appealing, wrapping around her like a warm blanket out of the dryer.

"Lawson."

"Would have been nice if John had mentioned this was your charter." His voice dripped with sarcasm.

"Wouldn't it just?" She dug in her purse for her wallet as Charles strolled toward her, either oblivious to the tension or outright ignoring it. She couldn't blame him for the latter. She extracted a twenty and pressed it into Charles' palm. "Thank you for the ride."

"My pleasure." He tipped his hat at her and walked toward the limo. She let her gaze follow him, anything to delay what she was sure would be the longest four hours of her life. When the limo door closed and the vehicle pulled up to the exit gate, she reluctantly turned toward Lawson.

He was within inches of her, and she sucked in a sharp breath.

"What're you about, Merilee? I'm sure this isn't a coincidence. From the way John was going on, I thought he had his balls to the wall over a demanding client. That you, princess?"

She straightened her shoulders and tilted her chin. "I requested you, yes."

"Well..." He drew the syllable out until it was almost two words. "Aren't I the lucky one?" He pulled his aviators out of his pocket and settled them on the bridge of his nose. His dark-blond hair was disheveled from the wind, sticking up in delicious disarray. Why was it the assholes were the ones who were always so good-looking? He stalked to her suitcase and withdrew a set of keys from his pocket. He unlocked the cargo door and tossed her bag none too gently inside. "This it, or is another limo coming along with the rest? Perhaps we should phone John and see if one of the larger planes is available."

The corner of her lip twitched at his juvenile behavior. If this was how he wanted to play it, fine. When he was trapped in the air with her, he'd have no choice but to listen. She made a show of studying her nails. "I may not be a pilot, Lawson, but my father *did* own this company. I know a thing or two about airplanes. I think you'll find the weight of my suitcase is within the safety guidelines for this Cessna." She pulled her sunglasses from her hair and put them on. "Of course, you would have had to have bothered weighing it to know that." She clicked her tongue. "How careless of you."

She turned her back with that remark and walked around the front of the plane to the passenger door. She bit back a smile. She really shouldn't goad him. She needed him, after all. But he had that smug, superior thing going on and she couldn't help herself. There had been a time when she'd thought Lawson had hung the moon, had literally pined over him, but those days were gone.

Merilee opened the door and carefully planted her stiletto on the narrow step above the landing gear wheel and hauled herself into the plane as gracefully as she could. Not that it mattered, as Lawson was now avoiding looking at her altogether. She pulled the door closed and pressed the lever to lock it.

The pilot's door opened and Lawson climbed into the plane, closing the door a little more firmly than necessary and jamming the lever into place. He pulled out his clipboard from the side of the seat. "So, to what do I owe this esteemed honor?"

No way in hell she was telling him now. He'd have her back on the tarmac with her suitcase in a skinny minute if she revealed her true purpose. "Just a vacation in Treasure Cay, Lawson. Not unlike your many other charters."

He snorted. "Visiting the flavor of the month I take it?"

She turned in her seat to look at him. A muscle ticked in his jaw as he adjusted the wing flaps for takeoff. He didn't seem to care that she hadn't answered him as he opened the window and yelled, "Clear." He started the propeller and the plane began to shake, the noise near-deafening in the small space.

Lawson already had on his earphones and pointed to hers. Once she had them in place, she heard his mocking voice. "Seems if you knew a thing or two about planes you would have put those on already."

She adjusted the mic and ignored him until he drawled in her ear once more. "So, am I right?"

She let out a long sigh. "About what, Lawson?"

"You headed down to see whatever man you've roped into providing you a distraction? From what, I'm not sure."

And there it was. She always suspected Lawson thought of her as a daddy's girl with no purpose in life. Dumping her business degree at the University of Georgia and heading to Julliard after her father's death might make her appear selfish. Leaving John in charge was probably looked upon poorly by the employees, but she'd only been nineteen, damn it. She rubbed her temple. "If you must know, I'm visiting my friend Elizabeth. Her parents own a home on the island."

"Of course." Lawson continued his preflight checks while she stewed over his reaction to her. It really shouldn't matter what he thought, but it did. That need for approval wouldn't be an ally for her when she talked to him about her concerns. She must remember that technically she was the one in charge. He was her employee, for now, and if her plan was successful it would stay that way, and she needed information he could provide. All this other nonsense didn't matter. "Law—"

"Peachtree clearance November 2-4 Charlie Sierra Tango has romeo information. We're IFR ready to copy."

She knew enough to keep her mouth closed from here on out. She could only imagine what Lawson's reaction would be if he had to radio back in if he missed something because she was jabbering. She listened as their clearance was read back and watched as Lawson wrote down every detail in surprisingly neat handwriting.

He tapped the pencil's eraser against the clipboard and continued ignoring her. "Ground, November 2-4 Charlie Sierra Tango is at Epp's Aviation, ready for taxi."

"Charlie Sierra Tango taxi to runway 2-0 right."

Lawson eased the plane onto the runway and pulled to the side to do his run-up. She'd watched her father do this countless times. Everything was so methodical, a synchronized system that was followed to the letter every time. Lawson pushed in the throttle and the plane shook with the effort. She eyed the gauge as the RPMs rose. He turned the yoke, looking out each window at the rudder. He continued on in his process and she could almost hear him ticking off items in his head.

He finally turned to her. So he hadn't forgotten she existed. "You ready?"

"As I'll ever be." She checked her seat belt and fisted her hands, tucking them under her thighs. She didn't like takeoff. Her knowledge of planes made her aware this was the most dangerous part of the flight. If he noticed her discomfort, he didn't say anything. Not that she expected him to.

For someone who acted so ballsy, Merilee seemed nervous. Whether it was from his uncalled-for behavior or the flight, he wasn't sure. John senior never mentioned his daughter being afraid to fly, so it must be the former. He'd try not to feel like an ass about it. He had his reasons for judging her as he did.

All her father had wanted was for his children to follow in his footsteps, to continue the business he'd built from his own sweat and tears. He'd given them everything and asked for very little in return. John Diego senior was the finest man he'd ever met. Hell, he was more of a father to him than his own waste-of-space alcoholic old man. That's why Lawson had gone military. It was a fast way out of the hell he was living in. And when his aspirations were shot down, John had been there to give him a chance.

The thought of John's own flesh and blood not respecting his one wish tore at Lawson's gut. His mentor had worked so hard to build this company for his children's future. But John was gone, his pain-in-the-ass son was in charge and Lawson was carting the princess around. He rubbed his jaw. "Tower, November 2-4 Charlie Sierra Tango finished run-up and we're ready for takeoff."

"Charlie Sierra Tango, stand by for clearance."

He looked at Merilee. Her fists were still under her thighs, her eyes were closed and she was breathing so heavily he could hear it through the headset. He prayed she wasn't a vomiter.

Since she couldn't see him, he took the opportunity to study her profile. She wasn't a spitting image of her father like John junior, so he could only assume her delicate features were a result of the mother who passed on when Merilee was just a young girl. She had high cheekbones and a small, upturned nose. Her father's heritage gave her olive skin and dark hair, but her eyes were sea-glass green, a definite gift from her mother.

He could remember the first time he'd seen them— he'd been in John's office when Merilee had excitedly entered the room, holding a thick envelope from Julliard. Her incredible eyes had sparkled with excitement, but Lawson had sensed distress in John senior. It became clear to him then just how much John longed for his daughter to work by his side.

She'd always been the one her father had faith in, and John had expressed his concerns to Lawson about his son's reckless behavior and apparent lack of direction. Getting John to complete college had been a feat in itself and Lawson knew John senior was counting on his daughter one day taking over. But she'd had other plans. That was clear when she took off like a shot after her father's death.

Did no one appreciate family and understand what loyalty meant? It was Lawson's own loyalty that kept him on with John junior, despite the miserable working conditions. He'd taught John all he knew, made certain the business was stable, and with only a small amount of regret had decided to move on. As much as he admired and loved John Diego senior, he couldn't sacrifice his own future forever. And honestly, it was John's children's responsibility to run Diego Charters. As much as he loathed John junior, he had to give the guy credit for at least realizing that.

Unlike some people…

Lawson jumped when static hissed through his earphones. "Charlie Sierra Tango, you're clear for takeoff runway 2-0 right, heading 1-8-0."

He eased the Cessna onto the active runway, pushed the throttle and started his takeoff run. Within seconds he had the girl airborne.

The minute the wheels left the runway, Merilee's left hand shot out and grabbed his thigh, her knuckles white.

Heat flashed straight to his groin and he inwardly groaned. A touch from the princess and his cock instantly hardened. This was an unpleasant development. All the bickering must have gotten his dick all riled up. Just what he didn't need.

He looked at her and her eyes were still closed, but she now had her bottom lip between her teeth. It was definitely the plane that had her so on edge. *Aw hell.* Even digging in deep for his inner ass wouldn't allow him to ignore this blatant cry for comfort. He placed his hand over hers, enveloping her fingers in his grasp. He gave a little squeeze.

Her head whipped toward him and she settled her gaze on his. She gave him a small smile of thanks before gently pulling her hand free, patting his thigh and twining her fingers together in her lap. His cock hardened all over again.

Aw, double hell.

CHAPTER TWO

Lawson's show of kindness was unexpected and unnerving. She was used to him being contrary, giving her the hairy eyeball and generally ignoring her at every opportunity. That knowledge was what had put her in a state, anticipating this trip and all she hoped to accomplish. Although she didn't understand it, his animosity had come to be expected so the act of compassion, albeit brief, had her somewhat discombobulated.

Okay, very discombobulated. And the spark of awareness that shot through her from his touch only added to her confusion. She didn't like this man. That had been established long ago. But she liked the feel of his hand on hers, liked his concerned gaze, liked what suspiciously looked like a bulge behind the fly of his trousers.

She'd always found him attractive. She wouldn't lie. But she didn't think she was unique in that way of thinking. She'd seen many women parade through his life before she'd left for Julliard. Christmas parties, family gatherings, he was always there. And always with a different woman. He'd married one of them and that lasted for about a year and then he was back to his usual shenanigans.

Flavor of the month indeed. He had some nerve accusing *her* of that.

She risked a glance his way. As much as she hated to admit it, especially having been around so many arrogant employees of her father, there was just something innately sexy about a pilot. Perhaps it was the precise control they had over such a powerful piece of machinery. And with Lawson it seemed effortless. The plane followed his commands, his mastery over it evident. Just thinking about it made her hot. But then she remembered this was Lawson. She frowned.

Atlanta Center disrupted her thoughts when they radioed a heading change for the Cessna. Now that they were in flight, she relaxed a bit. She glanced out the window and watched as downtown disappeared into the distance. It wouldn't be long before all she'd see below was a patchwork of land. And after their stopover in Ft. Pierce, when only open ocean stretched before them, she'd start the conversation. There'd be too many interruptions before then, she well knew. What she had to voice was upsetting enough; she didn't want to have to talk around air traffic control to do it.

"So how is everything going up in New York?"

14

Bored disinterest. That was the best way to describe his tone. But forced or not, she'd take him up on his offer of conversation. Stewing in uncomfortable silence all the way to their stopover in southeastern Florida wasn't an appealing option. "Good. You know I'm teaching, right?" She angled her body so she was facing more in his direction. He was studying the instruments and scribbling on his clipboard.

"Um-hmm," he replied, not looking her way. She fought the urge to flick him on the head. "John mentioned something about some school somewhere."

"Grayson Manor. In Manhattan."

"Manhattan," he droned. "Guess learning theatrical skills is important to rich kids."

And even more important to underprivileged children who don't have two dimes to rub together. Ass.

She crossed her arms over her chest and started to count to ten. She only made it to three. "Just what's your problem?"

He gave her his full attention then. How gracious of him. "No problem, princess." He waved one hand in the air as if dismissing some thought. "Just making an observation about your job."

She narrowed her eyes at him. "Seems more like you're making an observation about me. And a false one at that."

"Truth ain't always pretty, sweetheart." He smirked

15

before he switched the fuel tanks. "I just call them as I see them."

"Yeah, well, we all know your vision sucks."

* * * * *

It had been nearly an hour since she'd delivered her barb and he was still fighting the urge to laugh. Thank God she'd pulled a book from her bag and started reading because their conversation had nowhere to go but south. She was clever, he'd give her that. If he cared anything about Merilee, the remark might have stung. But he knew her type. Hell, he'd married her type. High-maintenance, selfish and full of venom when crossed. She was barking up the wrong tree if she thought her comment would get a rise out of him.

He glanced at his watch. About three more hours to go. He slid a look her way. She was staring at the horizon, rubbing her temple, her book abandoned in her lap.

A flash of green caught his attention and he leaned forward, studying the storm scope. He sighed. Thunderheads south of their destination. They stuck in a pilot's craw in the summertime. Popping up out of nowhere and acting as unpredictable as a rodeo bull out of the gate. Well, the silver lining to this thundercloud was the fact the trip would be shortened. They'd have to skip the stopover in Ft. Pierce to reach Treasure Cay before the storm, but that was fine with him. The sooner he got her to her destination, the better.

16

"Hey, Merilee."

She turned to face him and he steeled his expression for her icy glare. He was met with what could only be described as fatigued sadness instead. He studied her for a moment, waiting for her to say something, but she only looked at him.

"We, ah, are going to have to fly straight to Treasure Cay. Need to get ahead of some weather."

She nodded and turned toward the window, leaning her forehead against the glass.

Her behavior gave him pause. He thought of her father and was overcome with guilt. He really had no business being so rude to Merilee. Lawson ran his hand down his face. She was the epitome of all that irked him, but she was still John's daughter. A fact he'd lost sight of in his irritation. *Shit.* He'd be sure to apologize before they parted company. He knew he'd regret it otherwise.

Another hour passed and Merilee hadn't said a word. He must have pissed her off but good. Clearly conversation was no longer on the table. Lawson flipped on the pilot-isolation switch for the headsets. The least he could do was not interfere with her choice to avoid him. If air traffic control radioed him, he'd be the only one to hear it and she could continue to think about whatever was on her mind in peace.

He looked at the instruments. The storm activity was moving a lot faster across his scope than he was comfortable with. He'd put a call in to weather. Just to be on the safe side. They were still close to two hours out and if he had to divert them, he wanted to know sooner rather than later.

He frowned as he listened to the conditions near their destination. He looked at his scope again. A storm front had kicked up along the southern coast of Florida. *Damn it all to hell.* He was going to have to turn them around and head back to the States. There was no choice in the matter now.

He flipped off the isolation switch. "Merilee?"

She turned to face him with a reluctant look. "What?"

"Storms are moving way too fast for my taste. They'll beat us to Treasure Cay. I think the best thing to do at this point is to head back and put her down somewhere in Florida. Hopefully Ft. Pierce."

She wrung her hands together in her lap. Lawson fought the urge to settle the movement. His touching her would probably be the last thing she'd welcome right now. "Can't we just return to Atlanta?"

He shook his head. "I don't want to risk it. There's another front moving north through Florida."

Closing her eyes and leaning her head against the headrest, she mumbled, "Fine."

Lawson grabbed his clipboard and adjusted his mic. "Center, November 2-4 Charlie Sierra Tango needs to divert to Ft. Pierce due to weather." He listened as coordinates were given and read them back as he made notes in his log. He angled the Cessna back in the direction they'd come and as he turned to place his clipboard between their seats, he caught Merilee hastily wiping her cheek before turning her face toward the window.

Deep breaths, Merilee. You can't let him see you upset.

Well, her brilliant plan had gone all to hell like nobody's business. It was as if the fates didn't want her to talk to Lawson. First she got the frostiest reception in history back on the tarmac and now this abrupt change to their travel destination. What she wouldn't give if it weren't so. Time was ticking and she didn't have the luxury to postpone what she needed to do. But now what?

The phone call she'd received last week had instantly disrupted the happy life she'd created for herself in New York. She guessed her first mistake was trusting John felt the same way about the company as their father had. He'd been working so hard to learn all the ins and outs, after all, absorbing all the knowledge Lawson had to give. She should have suspected it was with an ulterior motive. When had John done anything without thinking of how it could benefit him? What she had thought was her brother ensuring their father's legacy lived on was truly just stuffing the pig before slaughter.

And now he wanted to sell. And apparently none of the employees knew.

She ground her back molars together. She'd been a fool to fall for her brother's game. Being so supportive of her theatrical dreams, telling her Daddy would have wanted her to pursue her passion.

Yes, by all means, Merilee. I'll hold down the fort. You've got to give this a chance. You'll never forgive yourself if you don't.

And off she'd gone. A naïve nineteen-year-old who'd just lost her father and thought she could count on her big brother to look out for her.

He looked out for her, all right. All the way to New York. And *out* she'd been, until Mr. Grimsley had phoned her with a few questions his client had about her perspective on the family business. Clearly John hadn't counted on the broker to contact her at all.

Her brother wanted out. And if she wasn't onboard with it, her only option would be to fork up half the value of the company from her inheritance and let John walk away. Then it would all be hers. But she wouldn't have a clue what to do from there. And so she needed Lawson. Desperately. She had a plan in mind, but if she didn't make a move soon her hopes of coming to some sort of agreement between the two of them before the shit hit the fan would be gone. And her brother hadn't given a rat's ass when she'd requested Lawson fly her. She supposed he didn't care how things went down. As long as he got his money.

She slid a covert glance Lawson's way. He was

talking through the headset and adjusting the instruments. His voice was smooth, controlled as he spoke. The Cessna made a short descent and then Lawson retrieved his clipboard and began making notations. It was now or never.

"Lawson, there's a reason I requested you for this flight."

He smiled at her briefly. "Aside from torturing me?"

His question didn't have his usual bite so she took it for what it was. A joke. Kind of. "Yes, aside from that."

"Okay, princess. What's on your mind?"

"I have some concerns and I need your input."

He raised an eyebrow and then held up his finger as static crackled over the radio. "November 2-4 Charlie Sierra Tango, be advised…"

Merilee pulled the headset from her head and dropped it in her lap. She snaked her hands into her hair. This was an exercise in torture. The whole damn flight. What had she been thinking, trying to orchestrate a business meeting this way? Clearly she lacked any sort of skill in that arena. She'd been a coward. Knowing her audience could be nothing but captive if trapped with her for a few hours. Served her right, really, to play out this way. Perhaps she wasn't cut out to run Diego Charters. Perhaps she should just go along with her brother, take the money and run.

No.

She wouldn't do that to her father. She may have gone

about this in an entirely ridiculous manner, but that didn't mean she couldn't follow through. She would just deal with this flight fiasco and arrange an immediate meeting with Lawson like a mature, capable adult. What she should have done in the first place.

Satisfied with her plan, she reached for her headset just as Lawson tapped her arm and pointed to it. She adjusted it over her ears and placed the mic in front of her mouth.

"What?" she asked.

"We're not going to make it to Florida."

Certainly she hadn't heard him correctly. "I'm sorry, what?"

His look was one of tried patience. "I said, we're not going to make it to Florida. Storm's moving up the coast too fast."

Merilee felt her heart in her throat and turned to look out the window. Ocean. Nothing but ocean. She swallowed down what felt like the beginnings of hysteria. "So, where else do you propose we land?"

"There's only one island this far north we have a shot at. Walker's Cay. Used to be a big diving and fishing destination before a hurricane blew it away."

"Blew it away?"

"Few years back. It's deserted now. They have a runway, but it was for shit when the island was up and running. The landing will be dicey at best." He reached

22

over and squeezed her hand. "Can you handle it?"

Handle it? Was he crazy? Who handles such a thing? She shook her head as if that could make it not so. "Certainly you can make it back to Florida. I mean, look. I see some sun over there."

"That's to the east. Storms are moving north and from our west. We'll get boxed in if we don't run out of fuel first."

Fear surged through her and suddenly losing her father's company paled in comparison to crashing to a watery death. "But can't you get to Florida? We haven't been out over the ocean for all that long, right?"

"A lot longer than you think. You were lost in your own world for over an hour."

She rubbed her temple. "But—"

The hold on her hand tightened. "Remember the pilot credo, Merilee? There are old pilots and bold pilots. But no old, bold pilots."

She nodded.

"And I plan to be an old pilot." He eased his hand from hers and tapped her gently on the thigh. "I flew to Walker's many times back in the day. I'm familiar with the runway. It's short, so it will be a bumpy put down, but I have confidence I can land us safely. Okay?"

She studied him for any sign he was lying, placating her before she met her Maker. He looked as assured of himself as always. She made the sign of the cross and wished for a rosary, although it had been at least a decade since she'd been to church. Certainly God would understand, right? "Okay," she answered on a shaky breath.

Merilee closed her eyes and clasped her hands together. Her nails bit into her palms as all manner of disastrous scenarios played through her mind. She tried to shake the thoughts loose. Lawson was a good pilot. The best Diego Charters had. They'd be fine. She drew a deep breath and looked toward him. He seemed unaffected and she took comfort in that.

She focused on happy thoughts. Sunshine. Puppies. Calorie-free doughnuts. Anything to keep her mind off the adjectives he'd used to describe the runway—short, bumpy, for shit. *Oh God.*

This wasn't the best scenario. Landing on Walker's nearly always shaved a year off his life, and that was before Hurricane Frances came through and destroyed the resort. The runway was short. Very short. And more than one pilot had gone right off the end into the ocean. That thought always crossed his mind every time he'd landed and listened to rubber screech across the pot-hole-puckered runway. He'd always landed flawlessly, and his clients never knew how his heart pounded or about the fact he said a little prayer with every landing he made.

He could only imagine what kind of shape the runway was in now. But that was the only viable option so he would just have to hope for the best. A crash landing was not the sort of thing he wanted on his record as he started his own company. And he certainly didn't want to leave such a blemish on the Diego Charters name. They had a perfect safety record. He would see that it stayed that way as long as he was officially employed there. Which he still was.

Lawson checked his coordinates and noted Walker's should be visible shortly. He looked at Merilee. Her eyes were closed and her fists had migrated beneath her thighs again. Every once in a while her lips would move as if she were speaking, but no sound came through the headset. She was probably praying. Not such a bad idea.

He drew in a deep breath and mentally prepared himself for the task at hand. Spying land in the distance, Lawson pulled out the landing gear lever and depressed it. The reassuring clicking sound let him know it was in motion. He looked out his window to check. He nodded and spoke to Merilee.

"Check out your side. You see the landing gear?"

"Yes," she said before resuming her same position—head back, eyes closed.

As they made their approach, Lawson was saddened to see the barren marina, the destroyed buildings. The island used to be packed with boats and visitors. Now it was silent. *What a waste.*

The Cessna made its descent, the runway rushing to meet them.

Wheels touched down and Lawson raised the flaps to reduce lift, applying the brakes.

The years had not been kind to the dilapidated runway and the Cessna skidded and dipped as asphalt abused the landing gear. A loud pop and the sound of grinding metal echoed through the interior as the plane neared the end of the runway.

Turning the yoke, Lawson veered into a grassy patch to the right of the runway…

Where the Cessna came to a blessed stop.

His heart nearly beat out of his chest when he realized they were down. They were safe. He turned to Merilee with a smile that faded as soon as he saw her face. It was as white as someone with her coloring could get.

He rubbed her shoulder. "We're safe. Everything's okay."

She nodded, taking a deep breath as she removed her headset. He did the same and placed it over the yoke.

"I thought we were going off the end." She looked as if she were going to cry but a strangled laugh escaped instead. She shook her head then glanced around. "You weren't kidding. That runway is short."

He opened his door to let air in. A stiff wind blew around them. The storm wouldn't be far behind. He'd keep how close they cut it to himself. "Yeah. I told you. Hop down. Let's look at the damage."

They both exited the plane and Lawson was relieved

to see the only damage to the gear was beneath the nose. Could have been a lot worse. Hell, he could be doing an emergency water evacuation right now. He would count his blessings. He patted the ladybird's side. "I should be able to fix this easily enough. Let's go find some shelter for the night and then once this storm passes through I'll be able to fix her up at first light. Then you'll be off to Treasure as planned." He turned to give her his warmest smile and felt it slide from his face when he saw her mutinous expression.

"Excuse me?" She stared at him, wide-eyed.

He scratched his head, wondering at what point in the simple sentence he'd lost her. "I *said*, let's find shelter for the night and I'll fix this first thing in the morning and then we'll be on our way."

"Here," she said, her tone indicating that any goodwill she'd had from him saving her ass was gone. "You suggest we stay *here*. All night."

"That's what I said."

She began to pace, her ankles wobbling as her spiked heels navigated the rocks and shells strewn throughout the grass. "Radio somebody. Surely there's someone nearby who can retrieve us by boat, right?"

"There might be, but we don't need to call for help. I'll have you to your destination tomorrow." He brushed past her and could very nearly feel her anger rolling off in waves. She could pout and fight all she wanted, but she was stuck with him until the morning. He walked to the tail of the plane and unlocked the cargo hold.

CHAPTER THREE

"So, you're really not going to radio for help?"

Lawson glanced over his shoulder just long enough to catch her outraged expression then went back to the task of planning the repair. He ran a quick mental inventory of what he had in his tool case. He could fix the wheel, but from the look of the angry clouds it would definitely not be until morning. He slowly rose to his feet and faced her.

"No, Merilee, I'm not going to radio for help. This is hardly an emergency."

"N-not an emergency," she sputtered, marching toward him. "We're on a goddamn deserted island surrounded by…" She spun in a circle. "Water!"

"Hence the term 'island'." He looked up at the threatening weather moving closer by the second. He let out a long sigh. "Merilee, go over to the customs building at the end of the runway. With any luck, it's unlocked. Wait for me there while I radio in and let them know we've landed *safely* on Walker's Cay and will be departing tomorrow, weather permitting."

"Are you serious?"

"Terribly." He raised his eyebrows and jerked his head toward the small white building behind her. "Go on, before the sky falls in. I'll be there in a minute."

She growled in outrage and stormed toward the old customs office. He tried not to laugh as one shoe's heel got stuck in a hole in the pavement and she strung together a melody of curses unlike anything he'd ever heard from a woman. She took off both shoes and continued on. He breathed a sigh of relief when he saw her yank open the customs office door and disappear inside.

After radioing in and setting a tentative departure time for the morning, Lawson grabbed his flight case and locked the door. He surveyed the position of the plane and was suddenly glad he'd run off the runway into the grassy area. He'd be able to tie her down there. He placed his case on the ground and leaned into the cargo hold. He withdrew two wooden stakes, rope, and his emergency kit and blankets. Once he'd cussed through the process of driving the stakes into the ground, he looped rope through the holds on the wings and securely tied the Cessna. Yanking on the rope, he was satisfied it would hold during strong winds.

Now his *patience*—that was another thing altogether. He doubted it would hold well at all once he joined Merilee. She'd gone from scared lamb to outraged lion in a split second. *This should be fun.*

Peering through the broken glass in the window, Merilee could see him trudging up the runway. Her momentary panic had subsided and given way to anger once she'd discovered what he was about. Not radioing for help? Was he insane?

She thought of his behavior for the last two hours. Insanity. Yes, that must be it. And this…this…*hut* he had her waiting in? This was a customs office? She harrumphed. This place had to be the equivalent of the sticks for the Bahamas. She'd seen closets bigger than this. *Office indeed.*

When Lawson was close enough to see her, she drew back and leaned her hip against the counter, attempting to affect a look of *put out yet in control.* The minute the door opened and she saw him, she had an immediate girly rush of being saved from sure peril and nearly threw her arms around him. She twined her fingers together instead. So much for not being a simpering female.

He placed his things on the counter next to her and gave her a concerned look. "You okay?"

Was she okay? Seriously? She was stuck with an idiot who was living out some manly survival fantasy at her expense. Daddy never would have let something like this happen. No old, bold pilots her ass. She put her hand on her hip.

"If you were concerned about my well-being you would have called for help. But no. Here we are like castaways from *Gilligan's Island*. Did you make yourself one of those fancy coconut phones for us to try to save ourselves with? Should we go spell out 'help' with palm tree fronds across the runway? Oh I know…" She poked him in his chest. "Find some bamboo and make ourselves a rickety raft to push into shark-infested waters."

Grabbing her fingers in his fist, he leveled his gaze on hers. "We're hardly castaways, Merilee. I'll fly us out of here in the morning."

She yanked her hand from his grasp. "But this island is abandoned. Has been for years. You said so yourself. What are we supposed to do, stay in this tiny shack with the holes in the roof until tomorrow?"

He shook his head and an amused smirk set up camp on his face. "It ain't exactly the Ritz, doll, but I think even someone such as yourself will be able to pull through somehow."

"What do you mean, *someone such as myself*? Do you think I'm overreacting to this…this adventure you've thrust upon us? Why for all that's good and holy can't you just call in for some goddamn help? Are you such a—"

Her head snapped back from the force of being pulled against him and before she could resist, the brute's mouth was on hers.

She braced her palms against his chest and tried her hardest to get some space between them, but the more she struggled the more demanding his kiss and the tighter his grip became. And when his tongue swiped the seam of her lips, she gave up fighting completely and surrendered to Lawson.

He was angry. She could feel it in his kiss. But that only made it hotter, heady. His tongue stabbed into her mouth, daring her to pull away, to refuse him entrance. But she wouldn't. Some part of her had always wondered what he would feel like. Taste like.

And now she knew. He tasted like sin. Forbidden and foolish and impossible to deny.

She wrapped her arms around his neck and threw herself into the kiss properly.

Lawson's guttural groan was her reward. He effectively boxed her in against the counter, his erection nudging her stomach. She slid her hands down his back to cup his ass and pull him more tightly against her.

He abruptly drew back. She looked up at him, dazed.

"Looks like I found one way to stop that venomous tongue of yours."

She couldn't have been more shocked if he'd thrown a bucket of ice water over her head. She pushed him away from her, cloaked in humiliation. He appeared unaffected by the kiss and she... Well, she was very much affected. Her heart still zinged behind her rib cage, and her nipples felt suspiciously erect. She crossed her arms over her chest. "Wh-what?" *Brilliant, Merilee. Babble why don't you?*

He gave her a half-smile oozing with smugness. Visions of clawing his face to shreds like a cat strung out on catnip filled her with sudden purpose. He may not like her much, but she wouldn't stand by and let him treat her like some common floozy. How dare he?

She cleared her throat. "Lawson, I really don't know why you seem to hate me so much and I really don't care."

Okay, so that was a lie. She did care. Very much. And wasn't that a bitch?

She drew a deep breath. "But I'd think you would have enough respect for my father to at least treat me with the courtesy you'd show a stranger on the street." She brushed past him and closed the short distance to the small window overlooking the ocean. Leaning on the windowsill, she peered up at the dark clouds moving toward the island.

She could feel him behind her before his hand rested on her shoulder.

"I'm sorry, Merilee. I was way out of line. I just couldn't listen to it anymore and…"

She turned at his hesitation and his hand fell from her shoulder to rest at his side. His gaze settled on hers and she was pleased to see he had the sense to at least look remorseful. Of course, she'd brought out the big-guilt-trip gun by mentioning her father. Low blow if ever there was one. But so fitting, considering. "And what?"

He ran his hand down his face. "And you're a very beautiful woman. I just reacted. I didn't think."

He thought she was beautiful? She had a moment of pure feminine pride before she once again remembered this was Lawson. Her moment deflated like a soufflé out of the oven too soon. Well, this was pleasant—being stuck here with him now that things had moved from uncomfortable to downright awkward. Which brought her back to where she'd been before he'd nearly had his tongue down her throat.

"You seem to have a reason for everything, so do you care to explain why staying put…here…is our best course of action?" She did her level best to keep all traces of sarcasm from her voice.

"Three reasons." He reached into a satchel and took out a bottle of water and handed it to her. She unscrewed the cap and took a swallow. "First, we aren't in imminent peril." She started to object and he arched one eyebrow. She took another sip. "Second, Diego Charters has a perfect safety record. No need to blemish it with a distress call that is unwarranted."

Shit. He was making perfect sense. Suddenly she saw herself as the princess he'd accused her of being. She cringed inwardly.

"And lastly, although you may not care one iota about this, I'd like to avoid the cost of an emergency call. Sending out boats and whatnot isn't exactly cheap."

His sensible words caused her stomach to drop to her

toes. Lawson never did anything without a reason, and she'd just made an enormous ass of herself by behaving exactly like the type of woman he perceived her as being. *Just great.*

She should apologize, say he was right, thank him for doing what was best for her family business. Something. She opened her mouth to speak but no words came. She watched the muscle tick in his jaw as he ran his hands through his hair and avoided looking at her. He dug around in his satchel again and pulled out the tennis shoes she'd packed. She sent him a questioning look as she took them from him.

"I grabbed these from the plane. I didn't think you'd want to walk around in those other shoes." He pointed to the stilettos she'd dropped on the counter.

She sighed. He was thinking of her comfort while she was acting like a brat. She slipped on the tennis shoes and laced them up.

Lawson went to the door and held it open. "Let's walk down to the hotel before this storm hits and see if there's any place in good enough condition for us to stay until I can get us the hell out of here." Merilee gestured to one of his bags. He shook his head. "I've got it. Come on."

Lawson cursed the weather to the pits of hell as he and Merilee made their way through the overgrown pathways that led to the main hotel from the runway. If not for the fucking storms, he'd be depositing Merilee on the tarmac in Treasure Cay right about now and flying away toward his new life. But no. Here he was on a deserted island with the princess.

Who had the softest lips he'd ever tasted.

And when she'd grabbed his ass and pulled him against her, he'd nearly lost his mind with need. He'd wanted her right there in that rickety excuse for a building—wanted to bend her over the counter and plunge himself into her welcoming heat. His dick was hard now simply from thinking about it. This was a complication he didn't need. The last thing he wanted was to *want* her.

But he did. There was no denying it. The way she sparred with him just turned him on even more. Kissing her had been the only thing he could think to do to stop her ridiculous ramblings. And when their lips had touched and she'd molded her body to his, he knew he had to stop immediately. And he did it the only way he seemed to know how with her. He'd acted like an ass. Used hurtful words to stop her in her tracks. Effective, no doubt. But he wondered now if he really *wanted* to stop her. Stop the heat between them. His body sure as hell didn't.

He glanced over his shoulder and saw her following behind, arms crossed, head down. Guilt consumed him. He shouldn't have touched her. It served him right to walk around with an erection because he knew just how responsive she was, how sweet her mouth tasted. How round and full her breasts felt pressed against his chest.

Damn, he was hard as fucking granite. This was going to be the longest night of his life.

"You okay back there?" he called to her.

"Fine." She sounded distracted. No telling what was going through her mind right now. If she was thinking about him, it was probably nothing good.

Lawson emerged from the path to what had been an open grass area lined by palm trees. Many of them had snapped in half, leaving a mangled landscape. He was happy to see the main building still stood. It appeared damaged, and most likely ravaged by floods, but it would at least provide them some shelter from the approaching storm. He stopped when he reached the pool area and waited for Merilee to catch up. He coaxed his erection into submission by thinking unpleasant thoughts, and by the time she reached his side he was mostly in control.

"Let's duck inside here and see what we're dealing with."

She nodded and trailed behind him. They entered the common area and he let out a long sigh. He had spent many a night here when he had a layover on the island. Seeing it abandoned and in such a state of disrepair saddened him. But it would do for shelter. There were a few holes in the pitched roof, and the door that led to the patio had boards where the glass used to be, but it was a sizeable room and they should remain dry. The seating area was still in the back corner as it had been years ago, but some of the furniture was missing. There was a leather

38

sofa and loveseat and a couple of upholstered chairs left, and he could use his blankets to cover them. Hopefully Merilee would be comfortable enough to sleep.

He turned to find her standing in the middle of the room, her arms wrapped around her abdomen. She looked small and frightened and he began to second-guess his decision to keep them here. Was he really helping them? He gave his head a slight shake. Yes, damn it. This was best for her too.

"It's not too bad," he hedged, walking toward her.

She turned and gave him a smile that seemed falsely sunny. "Nope. Not bad at all."

He expected her to make some snide comment but she didn't. He waited a few more seconds, but still nothing. "You hungry?" he asked.

"A little."

He walked to the bar and placed his bags atop it. "I've got some nutrition bars in here. That should hold us for tonight. I can probably catch some fish in the morning."

The corners of her mouth quirked up. "With what?"

"I can make a spear out of some driftwood. The shallows around this island are populated with all kinds of fish." Her smile grew. "What?"

"You really are getting all *Gilligan's Island* on me aren't you?"

He couldn't help but grin. "Well, you know the Diego Charters motto. 'We're not satisfied until our customers are.' I wouldn't want to disappoint you and have you report my ass."

She laughed and her cheeks flushed. Lawson chose to ignore the fact he found it adorable. That he found *her* adorable. "Um…" He scratched his head and then a thought hit him. "Oh shit."

"What?"

"I'm going to have to get back to the radio. Damn." He walked toward the door and peered out. The first fat droplets of rain were beginning to fall.

She joined him. "Why?"

"Your friend. Elizabeth. We need to get word to her that you'll be in tomorrow. Unless…" He pulled his cell phone from his pocket and stepped outside, walking a few feet from the lobby. He shook his head and returned to her side. "No signal, like I feared. Okay, you just sit tight. Give me her parents' names and I'll take care of it."

She muttered something under her breath he couldn't decipher and he leaned closer. "What?"

"Yeah, their name." She scratched her neck. "I don't have it."

"What do you mean you don't have it? What's Elizabeth's last name?"

She squared her shoulders and met his gaze straight on. "There is no Elizabeth. I lied."

CHAPTER FOUR

"Come again?"

"You heard me." She turned her back on him and took a couple steps away.

He let out a sarcastic laugh. "Yeah, I did. I'm just trying to figure out what in the hell you're talking about. No Elizabeth? What am I flying you for?" His thoughts drifted back to his first assumption and jealousy speared him. He couldn't figure out if he was angrier at her for lying or at himself for allowing her to get to him at all. As if he should care who was in her bed. "So, it really is the flavor of the month, huh? Any particular reason you wanted *me* to deliver you to his doorstep?"

She faced him. "There's no man, Lawson."

"Yeah, right." He placed his hands on his hips. "You expect me to believe you were just going down there all by yourself?"

"Whether you believe me or not, it's the truth."

He plowed a hand through his hair. "So all this is just so you can go off on some vacation alone? Don't you have any other way to amuse yourself?" He started to pace. "We're stuck here, with a damaged plane I might add, just so you can go off and laze around on some *goddamn* beach."

She met him in two long, angry strides, her hands fisted. "Stop making judgments. You don't know a damn thing about me! You think you do. But you don't. And I'm not responsible for the weather, Lawson," she spat. "This could have been any of your charters."

"Yeah, but it's not. It's you."

"Oh, I'm sorry," she said, her voice dripping with sarcasm. "I didn't realize flying me on a trip you make routinely would be such a hardship. Who knew you were so particular. Are you judgmental of all our clients or is it only me?"

She looked so indignant staring up at him. Her chest was heaving with her outraged breaths and he had a difficult time keeping his eyes off the hardened peaks he detected beneath the silk of her dress. He went instantly hard and his gaze shot back to hers. "You better watch it, princess. You're making me—" He clenched his jaw and took a deep breath.

"What?" she demanded, crowding him. A few more inches and she'd feel exactly *what* for herself. "I'm making you what? Please, pray tell."

42

Fuck. She had no idea what she was doing to him. And what he wanted to do to her. In every position possible.

"You're making me…hot."

He heard her sharp intake of breath and expected her to slap him or skitter off. He didn't expect her eyes to smolder and for her to stand her ground. Seconds ticked by in strained silence before she responded.

"So do something about it."

He was on her before she could change her mind. Before he could come to his senses. The rational part of him knew this was a mistake. But he wasn't thinking with the rational part of himself. He wanted her more than his next breath and if the way she yanked his mouth to hers was any indication, she felt the same way. Her lips were hungry, her hands seemingly everywhere at once as she groped him, pulling his shirt from his waistband and snaking beneath to his bare skin.

He reached behind her for the zipper on her dress and slowly drew it down, his knuckles brushing against the smooth skin of her back. She whimpered into his mouth, her fingers digging into the flesh of his abdomen. He gave her dress a gentle tug, letting it fall to pool around her feet. He pulled his mouth from hers and took a step back, his gaze raking over her. Her figure was lush and full, her narrow waist flaring out to softly rounded hips, which led to her mile-long legs.

And her tennis shoes.

He pointed to them and said, "Lose those."

She laughed and bent to unlace them and toe them off before she stood to her full height before him. Her olive skin was a delicious contrast to the white lace of her bra and panties—two other items of clothing he planned to dispense with as soon as possible.

Merilee seemed to have a similar agenda, because she wasted no time unbuckling his belt and ripping it from the loops. The button and zipper of his uniform trousers were the next on her list and she made quick work of freeing him from the confines of his pants, sliding them down his legs for him to step out. He nearly tripped as he fought to remove his dress shoes, but he righted himself and, as he stood, spied his good fortune—the front clasp of her bra. Easy access.

He popped open the closure and brushed the straps from her shoulders, grinning when she gasped as it fell to the floor.

If he thought her breasts looked magnificent wrapped in that scanty lace, that was nothing compared to the site before him now. He yanked her back to him, slanting his mouth over hers as she began to work on his shirt.

"Too...many...obstacles," she said between kisses, releasing each button.

"Standard Diego Charters issue, darlin'. You know that." He took great pride in the way he looked in his pilot's uniform, but he had to agree with her frustrated sighs. Too many damn buttons. He trailed kisses across her jaw and down her neck as he released the last of the buttons for her before shrugging the shirt from his shoulders and onto the floor. He groaned at the feel of Merilee's breasts pressed to his skin when he drew her flush against him. Lawson slipped his fingertips beneath the edge of the lace thong and squeezed her ass as he lifted her—no way to miss how hard and hot he was. Merilee wrapped her legs around his waist and moaned into his mouth as she began a torturous rocking motion against his cock. The material of his boxer briefs added friction with each stroke.

"Jesus, Merilee."

She nipped his bottom lip and he swore he felt her smile. If teasing was what she was into, he would gladly participate. He tore his mouth from hers and fastened his lips firmly around one nipple. He drew the taut bud into his mouth and sucked, sliding his finger along the curve of her ass until he dipped below the crotch of her panties. She was soaked, and he nearly came on the spot when she dropped her head back and groaned, "Oh fuck yes."

She had a mouth on her when she wanted it, that was for sure. But it only made him harder, more desperate to bury his length in her.

He eased his index finger through her slick folds, briefly circling her clit before pushing inside her channel. She was hot and swollen, bucking her hips in time to his thrusts. He gently bit her nipple and she hissed in a breath, taking one arm from around his neck to grab the weight of her breast in her hand. She squeezed the flesh, urging him to draw it farther into his mouth. He accommodated her, sucking and biting as he began to torment her in earnest. She rode his hand, moaning as each shift of her hips brought her closer and closer to release.

As much as he loved the taste and feel of her breast in his mouth, he had to watch. He focused on her face, the flush of her skin and the way she panted through partially parted lips. She was getting herself off, shamelessly humping him in erotic bliss. It was the sexiest thing he'd ever seen in his life. He curled his finger, searching for that spot that would—

"Fuck, Lawson!"

He felt her spasm around his finger as her entire body went rigid in his arms. She plucked the nipple he'd abandoned as she rode out her pleasure, gasping his name as her shudders subsided. She brought her sated gaze to his and he slowly withdrew his finger from inside her.

The musky scent of her arousal hung heavy in the air and he knew he had to have a taste.

Merilee watched Lawson's eyes drift closed as he sucked his finger into his mouth. The arm beneath her buttocks tightened as he groaned and drew on his digit, clearly relishing the flavor of her.

"You taste like heaven." He lowered her until she was

standing then hooked his finger through the waistband of her thong. He slid the lace down her thighs. "I want more."

He knelt and she placed her hands on his shoulders so he could help her step out of the thong. She expected him to lead her to the sofa she'd seen in the corner but instead he gripped her thighs and eased them apart. She sucked in a breath when his mouth closed over her clit. Her fingers dug into the flesh of his shoulders as she braced for what was sure to be another knee-buckling orgasm. She watched as his blond head moved between her thighs, her nails biting into his skin when he speared her with his tongue.

"So damn good," he murmured, and the vibration of the words against her clit shot pleasure straight to her core. He stabbed at the swollen bud with his tongue and she grabbed his head, drawing him away from her sensitive flesh.

"You're going to make me come. Again."

He grinned up at her. "Not like this I'm not. I want to feel you come around my cock, darlin'. Nothing else will do." He left a trail of hot, wet kisses along her abdomen, chest and neck as he slowly stood. He squeezed her hand before he stepped over to the bar and withdrew a blanket from his satchel, which he draped over his shoulder. He then grabbed his pants from the floor and fished in the pocket. He withdrew his wallet with a smile. She eyed him curiously.

"Condom." He pulled out a foil wrapper.

"Well, aren't you the ever-prepared Boy Scout?"

"Pilots are nothing if not prepared."

He stalked to her with what could only be described as male grace, a predatory look in his eyes. It so unnerved her that she spouted silly nonsense just to fill the charged silence. "Is this a service of Diego Charters I was unaware of?"

He grabbed her and laid a kiss on her, so hot it could incinerate panties—if she'd still had any on. "Hmmm," he murmured against her lips. "Not for clients, no. I'm simply trying to sleep my way to the top."

His joke hit closer to home than he could ever know. The panic she'd lived with recently rose to the surface but she forced the thought from her mind. The niggling anxiety vanished once he began to worship her breasts again. Just as she was getting well and truly boneless, he swept her into his arms and headed toward the couch.

She clung to his broad shoulders when he attempted to shake the blanket onto the worn leather cushion one-handed. Losing the battle with gravity, she plopped onto the sofa, pulling Lawson down with her. Her elbow bumped his jaw and he grunted.

"Sorry," she said, tracing her finger along the area of impact, her brow furrowed. He drew her hand away, tucking it between them. His gaze zeroed in on her lips. "Don't worry about it."

Lawson took possession of her mouth, his tongue driving inside to slide against hers. The steely length of him brushed against her center through his boxer briefs and she hooked her ankles around his back, drawing him closer. What was it about this man whom she was supposed to hate? He'd just made her come, quite well actually, and here she was again, on the precipice of another earth-shattering release.

Being with Lawson—in every sense of the word— could not be good.

An animalistic growl came from deep in his throat and his fingers dug into her hips. The sound alone nearly took her over.

Or it could be very, *very* good.

He stroked his erection against her as his tongue continued its sensuous caress of her mouth. Merilee pressed her fingertips under the waistband of his underwear and slid her fingers over his butt, grabbing the muscles as they contracted with each drive of his hips. Lawson tore his mouth away.

"Merilee." He panted, resting his forehead against hers. "You have to tell me no. Now. Right now. Otherwise…" He drew back to look her squarely in the eye. "This is probably wrong on about a hundred different levels."

She nodded. "Probably."

"And you'll probably hate me even more afterward." He traced the line of her jaw with a fingertip.

She bit her bottom lip and nodded. "Probably."

The crease between his brows deepened with that. "Hate" was not a word she'd currently use to describe the way she felt about Lawson Manning. Before she could tell him just that, he muttered, "Fuck it" and plunged his tongue into her mouth again.

Her body was thrilled with this progression of events. She was as slick with desire as she ever remembered being, the evidence of which was soaking his boxer briefs. She yanked them down his hips and struggled with her feet until she had nearly toed them off. He helped her the rest of the way, flinging them from his ankle onto the floor.

When his naked erection brushed over her pussy, all sorts of reckless thoughts hit her. Having him buried deep within her was suddenly more important than anything else. Luckily Lawson had the wherewithal to pause long enough to sheath himself, so she wouldn't be adding another mistake to her rapidly growing list.

But before she could focus on how reckless she was being, he slid inside and her world tilted.

The sound of her name on his lips as he drove home, in that delicious accent of his, was something she'd remember if she lived to be a hundred. The scratchy sound of it in his throat, the warm puff of air across her lips, his driving heat between her legs.

Perfect.

She arched her back as he thrust, creating the perfect angle. Each pass of his cock took her higher, closer to the peak of release. She groaned his name as the first tremors began to uncoil in her womb.

"I hope you're there, baby, because I won't last much longer..." Lawson slammed his eyes shut. "It's too much. You're too—"

She spasmed around him and he locked his gaze on hers as he drove his hips in powerful thrusts. Once. Twice. And then he was there, throwing his head back as he shook with release.

He collapsed on her chest, bracing his weight on his forearms. His breaths were ragged when he raised his head to look at her. A sense of feminine satisfaction stole over her when she saw how spent he looked.

She smiled. "I'm too what?"

He ran his hand into his hair, drawing a deep breath. He glanced over her head, a muscle in his jaw jumping. He met her eyes again. "Huh?"

Her afterglow started to fizzle when he didn't cozy up to her and answer her question. She was just playing with him, after all. She'd been known to go all girly after sex, though, so she pushed her insecurity aside. She cleared her throat. "You said I was too *something* right before you came. Don't leave a girl hanging."

He smirked. "It was nothing, princess. Just heat-of-the moment talk."

Princess? Was he serious? His cock was still buried in her and he chose that moment to revert to his usual unpleasant self? She'd clench his dick right off with her pelvic muscles if she were able. She pushed at his chest. "Get off me."

"Merilee," he said in a tone that screamed of forced patience as she scrambled out from under him and off the sofa. She spun around, taking a quick survey of the locations of her clothing. Her panties caught her eye and she traveled the few paces to retrieve them. She glared at Lawson as she stepped into the garment and dragged it up her legs.

She swept her dress off the floor and began to set it to rights. When Lawson heaved a sigh and tended to the condom, she turned her back to him. She bristled when she felt him behind her only seconds later. He gently brushed her hand away from the zipper she was practically ripping from the silk in her attempt to dress. He effortlessly drew it closed.

His lips brushed against her ear as he said, "Fucking hot."

She spun to face him. "What?"

"The end of the sentence in question was, *fucking hot*."

* * * * *

Lawson eased forward, being careful not to make any

movements that weren't absolutely necessary. He'd been at it for nearly an hour and didn't want to come back empty-handed. He was hot and wet and didn't have a thing on his spear to show for it.

Merilee's dislike of him had increased tenfold, he was sure of it. Which was exactly what he'd planned. As soon as he slid into her welcoming heat, he knew he was making a mistake of gargantuan proportions. If he'd been any sort of a man he would have ended it right there. Had the balls to do the right thing. But no. He'd gotten lost in all that was Merilee and his dick wouldn't back down. And he'd given in to that lust. Over and over.

He'd had some of the most intense sexual experiences of his life last night, but the morning shed light on what a boneheaded move it was. Thoughts of her father plagued him. John senior had thought of him like a son. What would he think if he knew how callously Lawson had treated his beloved daughter?

"Fuck!" Lawson snarled as the flash of silver evaded his spear yet again. He *would not* show up without food for Merilee. That was out of the question. He took a deep breath and drove his fingers through his hair. She'd looked so peaceful in her sleep when he'd checked on her before heading out to the flats to catch their breakfast—curled up on the sofa he hadn't dared ask to share with her. A broken lounge chair he'd retrieved from the bushes has been his bed. He'd dragged it inside the breezeway out of the rain. Perfect accommodations, really, for an ass such as himself.

Twenty-four hours ago he'd planned to make one last trip and kiss Diego Charters goodbye. Instead he'd kissed Merilee Diego—in multiple places. He went hard just thinking about it. And grew even harder when he remembered how many times he'd done a lot more than just kissing. Somehow he had to get through today. Deliver her to Treasure Cay and whatever, or whoever, was waiting on her, and then find some way to live with what he'd done.

That last bit was the kicker. He'd let John down. Something he never thought he'd do to his mentor. And in probably the worst way possible.

Movement to the left caught Lawson's eye and he went stock-still, watching the fish dart about. He slowly raised his spear and waited. With one powerful thrust, victory was his. At least he hadn't screwed up one aspect of this godforsaken fiasco.

* * * * *

Merilee eased her eyes open and blinked, bringing a strange room into focus. Her muscles ached. Her head ached. Between her legs ached.

She sat bolt upright. *Oh God.*

She'd fucked it up but good. Some businesswoman she was turning out to be. She was too afraid to just ask for what she wanted, and that cowardice had landed her on a deserted island with Lawson, instead of in a conference room with her proposal on the table.

Her nipples peaked just at the thought of him. Well, maybe she *was* able to ask for what she wanted…if it was Lawson between her legs. She'd managed to make that happen pretty damn efficiently. Her anger was no match for his charms and raw heat. One look from him and she'd surrendered like the hussy she apparently was. Multiple times.

She groaned and rubbed her temples. And then she'd done what any insane woman would do after such encounters. She'd procured a bottle of wine from an unopened case behind the bar and proceeded to drink most of it. Last thing she remembered was lying down for a few minutes before she had to woman-up and go find Lawson to apologize. He'd been an ass, that was for damn sure, but if it weren't for her idiotic scheming they wouldn't be in this mess in the first place. But she'd obviously passed out instead. She groaned again.

After a preliminary search, she spotted him in the shallows, appearing to make good on his promise of fishing. His shirt was off and the early-morning sun gleamed against his muscular back. He'd have scratch marks, no doubt, from where she'd scored her nails down his flesh when he made her come for the fourth time last night, after being a gentleman and making a nest for her on the dank leather couch. Hands down it was the best sex she'd ever had. With a man whom she thought she hated.

A man she *did* hate. Damn it…

Hate or no hate, she still needed him. And as close as she'd come to revealing all while draped across his chest in between rounds of toe-melting sex, she'd managed to keep her trap shut. In that, at least, she couldn't call herself ten times an idiot. But only in that.

Minutes, too many to count, ticked by as she watched him on the hunt. Then she saw him coming up the beach and dashed to her bag, hoping to quickly find her compact. She withdrew it from an inner pocket and snapped it open. *Shit.* About how one would expect to look after being stranded on an island with no amenities, sleeping on a scratchy blanket on a sofa smelling of fish, after being thoroughly tumbled. Lawson was as skilled with the female form as he was the planes he flew. Figured. Practice makes perfect.

She shook the disturbing thought from her head and tossed her compact in her bag, affecting her best fake smile as Lawson strolled through the door with his offering gutted on a stick.

"I told you there were fish and we'd have a decent breakfast." Masculine pride radiated off him in waves and she couldn't help but break into a genuine grin.

"That you did. That you did."

He eyed the fish briefly before giving her a skeptical look. "Any chance you know how to clean a fish?"

She wrinkled her nose and took a step back. "Um…"

He drew a deep breath and she couldn't tell if "princess" was on the tip of his tongue or not. She braced for the insult, pushing her shoulders back.

"No worries. Let me go for a quick swim then I'll clean the fish." He gestured toward the beach. It's a beautiful morning, why don't you take a walk? Breakfast will be ready in a few."

She eyed him for a long pause. So no insult, but no mention of the fact they'd been wrapped around each other like pretzels only hours before. She wasn't sure what was worse. She worried the long hem of the shirt he'd loaned her and nodded. "All right."

She went toward the door in what could only be described as a shuffle, confusion squeezing the life out of her like a python. Okay, she sucked as a businesswoman. That was painfully obvious. And apparently she sucked at being a woman also. She'd never dare to even consider herself a seductress, but for all that's good and holy, had the hot sex meant nothing more to him than a way to pass the time?

Cool sweat prickled her skin as she glanced over her shoulder to see him digging around in his pack, all his muscles completely at ease.

Well, okay then.

CHAPTER FIVE

The sooner he got this damn fish cleaned and cooked, the sooner he could get the plane fixed and leave this entire gut-wrenching experience behind. Watching Merilee walk by in his t-shirt, her legs tanned and feet bare, had his blood boiling—and not in the way he was accustomed to when it came to her.

She was a brat. A spoiled brat. He knew this. Her brother complained nonstop about how selfish she was, and Lawson had seen that for himself firsthand on numerous occasions. The way she'd skittered off. This so-called job where she apparently groomed other spoiled rich kids to overlook values in the pursuit of whatever they fancied. This trip she booked so she could sit on a beach somewhere while he and her brother worked to keep *her* family business going.

But his blood and other notable parts of his anatomy weren't quick to agree with his previous analysis. The woman he held in his arms last night was nothing like how he perceived her. She was attentive, passionate. Not just in it for herself. And when she'd lain across his chest, tracing circles with her fingernail over his pectoral muscles, he could see she was terribly deep in thought. If he'd been more of a man he would have asked what she was thinking. Damn. *If he were more of a man* had sure as hell started a lot of his thoughts since he'd picked Merilee up on the tarmac back in Atlanta. And the disturbing part was that the more time he spent in her company, the more he began to suspect he was *not* more of a man. Perhaps he was less of one.

Sure, he'd put his time in grooming John junior. Did the little bastard know a lot about running Diego Charters? Yes. Did he know enough? The answer to that question was the one Lawson pushed to the back of his mind whenever his conscience pricked to life. He did have a right to his own life. His own future. Hell, his own company. But the sad truth was, when it really came down to it, his business was Merilee's Julliard. He could stay on at Diego Charters under dickwad and do what he loved, just not how he'd love to do it. If he were honest with himself, he had to admit the same thought process could have occurred to her—despite her young age.

His thoughts continued down this path as he cleaned the fish and set it in his small cooler filled with ice packs. He had a driving need to see Merilee, to talk with her, and their paltry breakfast could wait a bit longer. He cleaned his hands with bottled water and hand sanitizer and went on a hunt for Merilee. There was very limited beach on the island, so she couldn't have gotten too far without having to turn back.

He'd only gone a few yards when he spotted her sitting in the sand, her arms wrapped around her knees, staring at the water. She glanced up at him when he approached before focusing again on whatever held her attention. He guessed it was merely her thoughts, as the water was a flat calm.

"Fish all ready?" she asked.

He dropped onto the sand next to her and sat cross-legged. "It's cleaned. I thought I'd come see what had your attention out in the ocean before I started the fire."

Merilee angled her body toward him, resting her cheek against her knee. "Nothing. Not even a fish or a bird. Just...nothing."

"I guess I scared them all off with my masterful hunting skills."

That caused her to smile, despite her apparent melancholy, and he noticed how it reached her eyes, crinkling the corners. "Must have." She looked away, taking sudden interest in a shell abandoned by a crab, which she rolled back and forth in the sand with her big toe.

Everything in him wanted to make sure that smile stayed on her face. It lit her from the inside out, and with his realization of how similar the two of them could be, she was utterly breathtaking to him. "Merilee."

When she looked over, he ran the tip of one finger along her cheek and then down her neck to rest gently against her throat. She swallowed and her heart beat like a hummingbird's wings beneath his fingertip, but she kept her gaze on his. He brushed his lips against hers, softly at first, but when hers parted beneath his caress, he plunged his tongue into her mouth. She whimpered and leaned into him, framing his face in her hands as she returned the kiss with vigor. Within seconds she was straddling his lap, rubbing against his erection.

Lawson hissed in a breath, digging his fingertips into her hips to control her movements. Too much more and he would come in his pants like an untried schoolboy. All because of her.

Because of *her*. Merilee Diego had him tied up in knots. He couldn't make sense of the two women battling in his mind. The one he always thought was selfish, and the one who ignited every need he possessed. He'd always called them as he saw them. But with her, that was no longer the case. He wanted to dig deep. He wanted to understand.

He wanted her beneath him so bad he couldn't see straight.

"I have to have you, Merilee." He brushed his mouth against hers, running his tongue along the seam of her lips. "Now. I have to have you now. Please say yes."

Say yes? She was already halfway there and he hadn't

put a finger on her yet. Not truly. And she sure as hell had said yes with gusto last night. What had changed in Lawson that he had gotten all respectful and shit all of a sudden? She drew back to look in his eyes. They were the stormiest blue she'd ever seen, but held traces of doubt. This man never doubted a thing in his life, as far as she knew. He never doubted what he felt about her. That was always abundantly clear.

She shook her head gently and started to extricate herself from his embrace. His grip tightened immediately.

"But you hate me, Lawson—"

"I never said I hated you," he protested.

She slammed her eyes shut. "Semantics. You don't like me very much. Like, not much at all. And last night must have been some sort of desperate attempt to just forget the current situation." She opened her eyes to find his brow furrowed. "I'm not so stupid as to believe it meant a damn thing to you."

"But what about you?"

Not something she'd expected to hear. A denial to lead to sex, yes. But an inquiry into what she was thinking? Not in a million years. And letting Lawson know his touch had affected her was not something she could share. Not something she *would* share. If she had a chance in hell of figuring things out and saving her father's company, she had to be smart. Stirring the pot with personal crap wouldn't help matters.

He stroked his hands down her back and cupped the globes of her ass. Good God. Well…she had to be smart about the *truth*. She would allow herself to be well and truly reckless with his body. He was offering it up like a goddamn buffet, so who was she to decline such an offer?

"Me? I want you."

Before she knew what he was about, he had her beneath him, all manner of shells and God knows what else digging into her skin. As if she could give a shit when he pushed the t-shirt over her head and off and started a wet, heated path to the edge of her thong. He grabbed the elastic with his teeth and pulled it down, down, down until her mound was exposed. She lifted her hips and he hooked the panties with a finger before flinging them away.

And then, God bless him, his mouth was on her. He made long, firm strokes with his tongue, always stopping on her engorged nub to suckle until she thought she might pass out.

She grabbed fistfuls of sand and threw it, writhing and carrying on in a manner that should have embarrassed her. A lot. Especially since this was Lawson Manning. But she couldn't find the resolve to not let him know just how hot he was making her, and just how desperate she was for him.

"Fuck me, Lawson. Now. Right goddamn now."

He laughed against her flesh and the vibrations made her growl in frustration. "You sure do have a mouth on you, darlin'. You know that?"

"Yes, and you know that too, so stop acting so fucking surprised and finish what you started."

Lawson had no idea where *this* Merilee had come from, but he liked her. A whole fucking lot. He was so hard he feared the damn thing might explode if he didn't bury himself in her hot sheath soon.

Between the two of them, they managed to unbuckle his belt and get his pants and boxers halfway down his legs. He reached for his wallet, and a condom, before they did away with them completely. Merilee got a predatory look in her eye before she pushed on his chest and forced him to change position. Once he was on his back, she snatched the foil packet from him. He reached for it, simply because he was certain the speed with which he could get it on would rival hers, but she waved it out of reach, smiling.

"Not yet, Casanova."

"Casanova?" he asked, eyeing the smug look on her face. "That's not very nice, you know. It implies I've been with tons of women. Which I have not."

She rubbed her very wet center over his erection. "But princess is fine, right? Implying I'm a spoiled brat only interested in herself?"

"Well, I—"

"Well, I..." she parroted him, adding extra sarcasm, which let's face it, he deserved. Merilee toyed with the condom, turning it in slow circles as her gaze bored into his. "You know, I guess I could just roll this on you and completely forget my original plan."

She looked so fucking hot straddling him with wicked intent in her eye that he started to leak pre-come. Whatever it was she was talking about, and he was pretty damn sure he knew what that was, he was onboard with.

"Okay, here's the truth," he managed to get out when she palmed the swollen head of his cock. "You're not a princess. And I'm…"

She stroked her hand all the way to the base, causing him to lift his pelvis. "Yes?"

"An ass."

"Fair assessment, I'd say." She licked her lips and his blood pressure went up about twenty degrees. "And since that honesty had to be painful, I'll do something very nice to make you feel better."

As she slid her excessively talented mouth and tongue over his erection, he did everything in his power not to wonder exactly why she was so good at it. Jealousy reared its ugly head, but was soon lost in the heat of her ministrations. With each upward pull she applied suction to his cock head, her gaze zeroing in on his face as she did so. He imagined he looked like a man so far gone he could go at any moment. He moaned her name on a long exhale.

Just as he was about to lose it, he grabbed her hair, probably a little rougher than he should have, and coaxed her up his body.

"Not like that, darlin'. As incredible as that was, I want to come inside you."

Lawson had learned he was wrong on many counts in the last twenty-four hours. He could now add being better at applying a condom to the list. Merilee ripped the foil with her teeth before pulling the latex from the wrapper. Even the way she held it in front of him was making him hot. She took the head of his cock in her mouth for one long, last caress before leisurely rolling the condom down his shaft, continuing to stoke the base as she did so. She took her sweet time with it, damn her. How embarrassing would it be to come while having a condom put on? Very, he knew, so he started reciting the military alphabet as she tortured his cock.

Alpha, bravo, charlie, delta...oh Jesus...echo, foxtrot, golf...fucking-A what was that?...hotel, india, juliet, kilo, mike, november...

Praise God, she had the damn thing on. She rubbed his dick through her wet folds. She moaned as she masturbated, using his cock, easing the head in an inch and then pulling out to circle her clit over and over again. Lawson settled into the sand and enjoyed the view. Merilee's hips rocked back and forth as she pleasured herself.

"Oh yeah," she said as she found a particular angle she seemed to enjoy. When she grabbed an ample breast in her other hand and began to pluck at the nipple, Lawson lost the ability to be a passive participant. He grabbed her by the waist and shifted their positions, pinning her beneath him. He thrust in to the hilt, knowing he'd never again feel this sexually satisfied even if he lived forever.

Her hot, tight passage wrapped around his erection, her breasts bounced with each rough thrust, and her eyes... Their smoldering depths wrecked him. This was not casual. No connection like this could be. And that scared the hell out of him.

The look in Lawson's eyes changed on a dime. They went from reflecting a man intent on fucking her brains out to something she couldn't quite put her finger on. But when he leaned down and kissed her, slowing his thrusts so he could worship her mouth, she found she didn't care what the reason was. Lawson felt right inside her, on her, around her. And no matter what came of them after this trip, she would always remember him in this exact moment.

He clasped their fingers and held her arms above her head, causing a delicious rasp of his chest hair against her nipples. He kissed her deeply, nibbling her lower lip and then sliding his tongue against hers.

"You're so beautiful," he whispered before pressing kisses across her cheek to her ear. "I never knew how much."

She was turning to absolute goo. The dynamics of this roll in the sand had taken an abrupt turn. And she knew he felt it too. What in the hell she was supposed to do about it, she had no idea. So she did the only thing she could do—rode out the ecstasy.

He let go of her hands to reach between their bodies, seeking the bundle of nerves that would send her over in a heartbeat. A couple brushes of his thumb and she was there, wrapping her legs around his hips and screaming his name. Two more thrusts and he joined her, his chest heaving as he spilled his seed in the condom.

They held each other as their breathing returned to normal, then Lawson slowly rolled off her. He removed the condom and proceeded to dig a hole to deposit it in. She slapped him on the shoulder.

"Do you have a better suggestion? And besides, that's how they did it on *Gilligan's Island*, you know."

She laughed, holding her belly. She loved this Lawson.

No, she *liked* him. That's what she meant. This was a part of him she'd never witnessed, the sex aside, and she was kind of digging it. It was no wonder, really, her father had loved him so much. As much as it pained her to admit, the man did have some redeeming qualities. Working the female body as if he were born to do it currently topped her list.

They put their clothes back on in silence and took a seat next to each other. Lawson kicked sand onto her foot, slowly burying it. He leaned into her, nudging her shoulder.

"So...I figure that after we eat and load up the plane, it'll take me about an hour or so to repair the damage to the front wheel and then we'll be able to—"

Merilee followed his line of vision over her left shoulder and frowned. Angry storm clouds loomed in the distance, the sunny morning that had lifted her spirits before Lawson had come out and rocked her world deserting them. Just like her brother and her opportunity to save her father's company. She sighed before meeting Lawson's eyes.

"Let me guess. We're not going anywhere."

Lawson ran his hand down his face. "I'll have to head back to the radio to call weather, but those clouds don't look promising."

Merilee groaned aloud, frustration coiling at the base of her spine and radiating through her body. As much as she had enjoyed the last few hours of bliss, despite their circumstances, this was not reality. Reality was a conversation she couldn't put off much longer. Feelings were beginning to muddy the waters, at least on her part, and although she didn't know a lot about business, she knew propositions of a professional nature didn't belong anywhere near the bedroom. Or a musty old couch or abrasive sand, as the case may be. She needed to pull on her big-girl panties before things got more...involved.

"Did you hear me, Merilee?"

She jerked her head up to find him looking at her with concern etched on his forehead. In that moment, she knew her feelings were more than muddied. She had screwed up nice and fine, allowing simmering affection she'd secretly held for Lawson from the get-go to surface, suffocating her in a haze of lust and indecision.

"Oh, sorry. No. I was off in my own little world for a minute there."

He studied her for a moment, narrowed his eyes, then his face relaxed. "I asked if you were okay waiting for breakfast until after I check weather."

"Of course." She waved him off. "No rush."

He reached for her and gave the top of her head an awkward caress. "All right. I'll be back soon."

She watched as he trudged through the sand toward the main lobby, admiring the play of muscles in his back. A steady throb between her legs reminded her of how capable that magnificent body was. Damn, she would miss that when all this was over. And depending on what information Lawson was about to receive, that could be very, very soon. She best get her wits about her and start thinking with her brain, not her hormones. Or, God forbid, her heart.

The way she saw it, she had one opportunity left to plead her case. If storms were rolling through, it would be on that dilapidated couch. If he got the all clear, it would be in the air. But either way, she had to do it, even if she had gone and fucked everything up by opening herself to Lawson.

Good job, Merilee. Now you have two things to lose. The company and your heart.

CHAPTER SIX

As Lawson made his way through the weeds and overgrown shrubs back to the main lobby, he questioned his sanity. Storms were moving through. And he was damn happy about it. Yesterday, he couldn't drop the princess—no, Merilee—off on Treasure soon enough. He had itched with the need to unload her spoiled, ungrateful ass from his plane and from his life. And now his treacherous dick was hard as steel at the thought of another night with her.

And even worse? His treacherous heart was onboard also.

He'd uncovered a side of her he never knew existed and it had softened his opinion of her dramatically. He was ashamed to admit that side had probably always been there, he just never took the time to look past his own opinion. And shame on him. John senior had worshipped the ground she walked on. There had to be a reason for it.

One thing was for sure. He was learning a hell of a lot

about himself on this little adventure. And he wasn't liking what he'd found. Somewhere along the way he had become even more jaded than he realized.

But soon this would all come to an end. He'd take Merilee to her destination and get on with his life. He knew that however different she seemed, she was still Merilee Diego. Resident of New York. Chaser of dreams. And despite the few similarities they shared, he still had no doubt he was only a passing amusement for her. There had been too many opportunities in the past for him to pick up on any affection on her part.

He could blame this entire scenario on chemistry. It was a powerful thing. And the added adrenaline from nearly screeching off the runway only added fuel to the fire. Molten-hot sex was inevitable. And if he were lucky, it would be inevitable again tonight.

Merilee was nowhere to be found when he entered the lobby. He knocked on the bathroom door, but there was no reply.

Then he smelled it—the distinct odor of wood burning. He followed the scent outside and found the woman in question feeding bits of driftwood onto a very healthy fire.

"Color me impressed."

She jumped at the sound of his voice and then smiled. "John junior wasn't into camping and Daddy loved it, so…"

"You went with him." Lawson crouched in front of

the fire, surveying its construction. It would burn for quite a while.

A wistful look came over her face. "We did everything together. Except fly. I tried many times, but would panic." She gave a self-deprecating laugh. "How sad is that? My father owned a charter business and I couldn't bring myself to take the leap and pursue a license."

Lawson saw true remorse on her face and remembered her fear at takeoff. He scooted around the fire and took a seat next to her. "Don't be so hard on yourself. Your brother can't fly, remember?"

Anger flashed in her eyes for a brief moment before she banked it and looked away. "But Daddy wanted me to do it. And I couldn't." She heaved a weighted sigh. "I thought about giving it another go the summer after my freshman year at Georgia, but then, well…"

Her father died. And she left.

Lawson reached for her but she stood abruptly, turning her head as she swiped at her cheek. "So, where's your big catch? Let's get breakfast started. I'm starved."

Her body language screamed he'd get nothing more out of her, so reluctantly he rose and walked to the bar where he'd stashed the fish. A quick search through the overhead cabinets scored him skewers. He'd attended a few of the Monday-night bonfires during layovers, and he remembered fondly cooking whatever catch the fishermen had brought in that day.

He joined Merilee by the fire, cooler in one hand. "Voilà," he said, waving the box of skewers.

"Lucky break," she mused.

He placed the cooler in the sand. "Not really. This isn't my first time cooking out on the island. It was a weekly tradition for guests."

"Ah, I see. And here I was getting all impressed." She grinned down at him as he crouched and speared chunks of fish.

He handed her a skewer and prepared his own, trying to think of a witty remark, but all he could come up with involved her on her back and him buried deep in her heat, showing her just how impressed she should be. He settled for a warm smile instead.

She sat cross-legged by the fire, slowly turning her fish. "So, bad news on the weather, I take it?"

That depends on your perspective. "Um, yeah. There's another system rolling through, but it should be out by tonight. I'll work on repairs before it hits, that way I can get us on our way early in the morning."

She nodded, frowning at her fish. He would give just about anything to know what was going on inside that beautiful head of hers. Whatever it was, it was heavy. But he had no right to it, he knew. A few rolls in the hay didn't grant him an all-access pass to Merilee. And with the way he'd treated her over the years, he didn't deserve it anyway.

They ate in companionable silence until every last bit of his hard-earned catch had been consumed. He tossed his wooden skewer into the fire and stood. "Well, I'm betting I have about an hour or so before the sky falls in again. I'm going to head back to the plane and get to work." He offered his hand and she took it, pulling herself up to a stand. "Want to join me?"

She shook her head. A little too fast for his ego. "Are there any berries or other fruits you know of on the island?"

Lawson rubbed his chin, heavy with blond stubble. He'd tend to that later. "If I recall, there are a few banana trees, and they often had fresh berries at breakfast. Whether they came from the island or not, I don't know. But the hurricane could have destroyed it all."

She bit her bottom lip, and his cock surged to attention. He suspected he'd stay in that state until they parted ways. That should be comfortable.

"I'd like to take a walk around the island and look. It's the least I can do after your prolonged fishing expedition this morning."

"Prolonged?" So she must have woken sooner than he'd thought and caught the full show. Complete with awkward misses and colorful language.

She broke out into a full smile then. "It was quite entertaining. Gilligan."

He narrowed his eyes at her. "Watch it, sweetheart. Or I just might leave your delectable ass here on the island."

Her eyes became a stormy green and his dick jumped for joy. But his brain won out in the end. Damn it all to hell. "I'll be back in an hour or two, weather permitting."

She saluted him and he laughed as he went into the lobby to grab his shirt and pack.

Merilee watched *his* delectable ass as he disappeared into the lobby. Every fiber of her being had lunged at the opportunity to go to the plane with him, visions of climbing onto the Sherpa-lined seat and rocking the plane until some other part of the machine broke off forefront in her thoughts. But she had to get her shit together. This sexual detour was scrambling her brain, and if she wasn't careful, she could lose everything over twenty-four hours of mind-numbing sex. She should be talking. Not spreading her legs and riding him like a pogo stick at every opportunity.

The fact she had no idea how he would take the news still terrified her whenever she thought of it. He'd never taken her seriously. Why should he now? Why should he believe she wanted to save her father's company above all else? He had no idea what John junior had planned, that much she did know. No one did. Her brother had been very careful about that. A few phone calls to several employees about a Christmas event she pretended to plan verified that information. Not one person let on that they might not be there come Christmas. Only her bastard of a brother would know that could be the case.

Unless…

Unless she gained the aid of Lawson to help her run the company and bought her brother out with every last dime of her inheritance. She knew he wouldn't care where the money came from. As long as he got it.

Merilee dug her fingers into her hair and pulled until her scalp burned. What a fucking mess. She surveyed the area beyond the lobby and figured that was the best route for her fruit-hunting expedition. She'd need to empty her bag to take with her, in case she lucked out and found something edible, and she'd use the solitude to iron out her plans. She'd broach the subject with Lawson tonight and hope for the best. There was nothing else to do at this point.

* * * * *

Merilee had no idea how long it had been, or how far she'd walked, when the first fat droplets of rain began to pelt her. She looked in her bag at her pitiful collection. She'd found one blueberry bush and pulled off every healthy berry she could find. Which wasn't a lot. The hurricane had, in fact, snapped most of the banana trees in half, but she managed to find a couple that had withstood the winds and had some fruit on them. The bananas were as green as Kermit and hard as a rock, but if they were desperate, the fruit would be edible.

She turned in a circle, trying to figure out which direction led to the hotel. After a minute or two she got her bearings and started the trek back. Not much ground had been covered when the wind accelerated and the sky opened up, dumping rain so rapidly the drops beat down on her. She searched for shelter of any kind and found a copse of trees near the beach and darted over to stand below the leafiest one, where she merely got wet. Not soaked to the bone.

Merilee leaned against the trunk with an agitated sigh, plucked a blueberry from her bag and popped it into her mouth. Not half bad. Reaching for another, she resigned herself to waiting out the worst of the rain before she headed back. She hoped Lawson had already returned and wasn't stuck also.

* * * * *

Lawson dashed the last few yards to the lobby just as rain came down in a violent deluge. He stepped inside and shook his head, water scattering across the floor. When he'd checked weather again while working on the plane, he'd discovered the bad forecast had been upgraded to a severe line of storms with heavy lightning. The last place he wanted to be for that was on an island, in the middle of a wide-open space, working on a huge mass of metal. A loud clap of thunder sounded and he let out a relieved breath. He and Merilee would be fine in the lobby until this passed.

He dropped his pack on the bar and looked around the room, expecting to find Merilee on the dilapidated couch. When he didn't see her, he wandered toward the office area in the rear of the building. There had been a small library of books near the reception desk and some staff quarters that wrapped behind the main bar lobby. Perhaps she'd gotten bored out of her skull after her fruit expedition and had wandered around the building.

"Merilee?" he called as he walked toward the office. The library turned up nothing, so he headed to the staff quarters. After looking in each of the five rooms and finding them empty, he began to worry. *Where in the hell is she?* The chapel was completely destroyed by Frances, so that wasn't an option. And they hadn't dared venture to the three-story hotel, as it appeared to be near collapsing. Merilee was a smart woman. She wouldn't have gone there. So that left one option—she was still out searching for fruit.

Fear for her well-being gripped him and he ran back through the lobby and outside. The island was only a mile and a half in circumference, but with bolts of lightning popping around him, the hunt would be treacherous. He took off toward the area of the island with the thickest vegetation, figuring that would have been the direction she'd gone.

He'd been running around calling her name for ten minutes with no luck. Of course, the loud clashes of thunder weren't helping matters much. He saw trees off in the distance and took off like a shot, praying like hell he found her soon. Terrible scenarios were running through his brain and he was in a near panic when he caught a glimpse of blue against a tree trunk in the distance.

"Merilee!"

The blue moved and he saw her peer around the tree. "Lawson?"

Thank God.

He dashed toward her, chanting *sweet baby Jesus* in his head over and over as lightning streaked all around him. When he reached the shelter of the trees, her eyes grew wide.

"Good Lord, Lawson. You're soaked to the skin."

He bent over, resting his hands on his knees as he heaved breaths in and out. "You think?" He couldn't help the sarcasm.

The corner of her lip quirked. "So, what are you doing, running around in the storm like an idiot?"

I'm the idiot? "Oh, I don't know, Merilee. Coming to save you and keep you from getting electrocuted?"

A delicate eyebrow rose. "Save me? What did you think I was going to do? Find a piece of metal and stand out in the open, waving it around? Harness some energy to fuel our rickety raft and coconut phone?"

Had she just mocked his heroic rescue effort? He pushed wet hair off his forehead and eyed her from head to toe. She didn't look too damsel-in-distress-ish. In fact, she looked cool as a cucumber, if not a little wet.

"I didn't like the fact you were out in the storm. I didn't know where you were."

Both her eyebrows shot up with that statement.

Why don't you tell her how you really feel, dumbass?

"I'm touched you were so concerned. But as you can see, I was smart enough to find shelter. I'm a lot safer from lightning under here than I would be running around out there."

And *he'd* dashed out without a second thought. He knew Merilee was intelligent. But something primitive drove him to find her. Make sure she was safe. And that same primitive instinct was on high alert now, knowing she was fine. In a t-shirt clinging to her full breasts.

What in the hell was the matter with him? He'd never been so all over the place in his life. And all because of this one woman.

"I was— I just thought..." He gnashed his back molars together. "Aw, fuck it." He grabbed Merilee and hauled her against his chest, cutting off her gasp with his mouth.

He plunged his tongue in deep, digging his fingers into her shoulders to hold her in place. Her shock soon turned carnal and she wrapped her arms around his neck, allowing him to lift her so she straddled his waist. He backed her to the tree trunk and they groaned in unison as his hard length rubbed against her. With one hand, he pushed the blue skirt up around her waist. His mouth latched on to a nipple through her tank top and she writhed against him, moaning his name. Thunder and lightning roared around them and he couldn't give a flying fuck. His only objective at this moment was sinking his cock into her heat.

She burrowed her fingers in his hair and yanked his head back, crushing his mouth with hers. She ground her pelvis against him and from her breathing, he knew she was close. But he wasn't going to allow her to dry-hump her way to completion. Not when he had an aching erection that could do it for her. With haste, he undid his trousers and slid them down his hips. A quick brush of his fingers and her panties were pulled to the side, his cock head gliding over her slick heat. Wet, so wet.

"Come on, Lawson. Do it," she said against his mouth. "Fuck me."

He was about to do just that when his damn conscience took over. It took every ounce of restraint to not thrust home. His fingers dug into her hips, holding her still. "No condom. We have to—stop."

Her breathing was harsh as she looked into his eyes. He saw different emotions flicker through and he prepared to gently lower her to the ground. But as he shifted her weight she grabbed both his wrists, stopping the motion.

"I'm on the Pill. I trust you, Lawson." His heart skipped a beat at her admission. "I can, right?"

She was so vulnerable in his arms, putting it all out

there. Her desire. Her trust. Did he deserve that? He wanted to. She continued to study him, unease radiating off her. She broke eye contact, but he returned her gaze to his with a gentle nudge of her chin.

"Yes, Merilee. You can trust me."

He kissed her with all the newfound emotion he was feeling. He didn't understand it, but he certainly wasn't going to fight it right now. Not when she moaned against his lips and rocked her hips toward him. With one quick movement he was buried to the hilt, wrapped in her tight sex. He allowed her to take control, ride him to completion. When she tumbled over he began to thrust in earnest, each plunge drawing him closer. He groaned her name as he came, wrapping her tightly in his arms.

He pressed kisses along her throat, pausing at her pulse. It hammered in her veins, much as his did. He gently withdrew from her body and placed her on her feet. He suddenly realized the thunder and lightning had passed, but a storm of an entirely different sort had started.

He was falling for Merilee Diego. Hard.

CHAPTER SEVEN

Merilee broke off a small bit of chocolate and passed the bar to Lawson. The sun had set an hour before and they were cozied up by another fire of her making. She'd decided the time had come for her to woman-up and lay a groundwork of questioning to lead toward her goal. But Lawson had used her innocent queries as a means to tease her, roping her into a game of truth or dare. Not that it was an altogether unpleasant experience; she was just getting nowhere fast.

"Okay, Lawson. Truth or dare?"

He gave her a sinful grin. Much like all the others he'd bestowed upon her since they'd started this game. "Dare."

She'd indulged him up to this point, and there had been a lot of stripping and oral sex going on. There hadn't been a truth in the mix at all. But game time needed to be over. "I dare you to take *truth* instead."

He smiled at her. "Clever game play, sweetheart. Are

you tiring of my tongue between your thighs?"

Her entire body heated at his response, but she stayed the course. "Who could ever tire of that? I just thought it would be fun to mix things up some."

He studied her for a long moment, as if he were trying to figure out what she was up to. If he only knew...

"All right. I'm game. Truth, then."

A cold sweat broke out on her skin as she formulated the best way to get the conversation rolling toward her goal without just blurting the whole mess out. Her attempt half an hour ago had fallen flat.

And then inspiration struck. Lawson had made it crystal clear when her father was alive that he wanted to work alongside him, hopefully running Diego Charters one day. She had no idea if that were still the case, but she would approach it from that angle, leaving out the part where John junior would be gone and she, helpless and ignorant of the day-to-day operations, would technically be his boss. Leaving most of the work for him. At least initially.

She rubbed her hands together. "Okay, truth. If you could have any job you want, do anything you want, what would it be?"

Her heart raced as she awaited his answer. He could either make this very easy for her or very difficult. Her hope plummeted when he didn't answer right away and instead took a keen interest in the chocolate she'd handed over. He placed it on a rock next to him and turned so he could face her.

"I actually have some news. I figured your brother would tell you later, since I didn't expect to see you, and then with all that's happened it wasn't on the top of my list to worry over." He gave her a half-smile and she knew she wasn't going to like what she was about to hear. No way, no how.

She forced what she hoped was a genuine smile on her face and drew a deep breath. "Good news, I hope." Boy, did she ever.

"I think so." He ran his fingers through his hair. He looked way too uncomfortable for her liking, and her instinct was to put her arms around him. But she was paralyzed by icy fear. "Um, as you know I've been working with John for five years now, teaching him all your father taught me." He smirked. "Or trying to at least."

She nodded numbly. Her cold sweat had graduated to an all-over prickling sensation.

"Anyway, the last three years or so I've been getting kind of restless. And aside from the irritation of dealing with your asshole of a brother..." He gave her a sheepish grin. "Sorry, but I call them like I see them."

"I know. And in this situation you're spot-on."

"Unfortunately, yes. But again, aside from dealing with him, things just didn't feel right. Like they used to when your father was alive. My goal had always been to make a success of myself, as he did. I feel I owe it to him, after all he did for me, you know?"

A glimmer of hope began to unfurl in her chest. Yes. *Yes.* Her father would want that. And what better way to accomplish it than to, for all intents and purposes, be the leader of Diego Charters? She may technically be the owner once she bought out her brother, but let's face it, it would be all Lawson Manning. She was about to say just that, reveal John's ugly truth, when Lawson continued.

"I've been saving most of my pay for the last few years and was able to purchase my own plane. She's not shiny and new like the planes your father would buy, but she's mine. And I know that by starting my own charter company, specializing in Caribbean destinations, I'll be making your father proud. He started from the ground up, and from his wisdom and encouragement, I'll be able to do the same." He reached out and tucked her hair behind her ear. "What better way to honor his memory, right?"

Her blood ran icy through her veins, her heart galloping in fear. He was leaving Diego Charters? John obviously knew that. The rat bastard. He really did have her against a wall. Without Lawson, she didn't have a chance in hell of keeping their father's company up and running. She was no pilot. She was no businesswoman. She was…screwed.

Tears pricked the backs of her eyes and she did everything in her power to keep them at bay. Sure, she could beg and plead to Lawson. And he might even cave.

But then she'd just be the selfish princess he'd accused her of being. And she refused. The last twenty-four hours had changed everything. Lawson had a piece of her heart. And she would not break his by trying to steal away his dream.

"Merilee, are you okay? I know this is probably a surprise to you, but I couldn't stay on forever. Diego Charters belongs to you and your brother. And John, despite all his flaws, has worked hard to continue to build the company with my help. Annual revenue has increased by twenty percent over the last two years. You'll be in good hands."

She drew a deep breath and was mortified when a small sob escaped her lips. She tried to cover it with a cough but it was too late. Lawson put his arm around her shoulder and pulled her firmly against his side, gently kneading the muscles in her neck.

"I'm sorry I've upset you. I had no idea you would care one way or the other." He kissed the top of her head. "You going to miss me, princess, or am I just an arrogant bastard to think your reaction is because of me?"

He tried to coax a smile out of her and she drew on every bit of strength she had, her lips tipping up at the corners. "It's partly you," she lied, "and partly my dad. Talking about him like this is just a painful reminder he's gone."

He pulled her onto his lap and held her against his chest. "I know. I miss him too. But he wouldn't like all this sadness." He playfully jostled her. "Let's continue our game, because I have a depraved dare I think you'll be totally onboard with. And then, after a good night's sleep, I'll finish those repairs and have you in Treasure Cay in no time. And you can continue on with your plans."

But she couldn't really. Her hopes and plans were as dead as her father. She only hoped she could live with falling short once again.

"Truth or dare?" he asked, brushing his thumb across her nipple.

Well, if there was anything that could take her mind off the disaster that was now her life, it was Lawson's ability to make her a desperate, craving wanton in ten seconds flat.

"Dare."

* * * * *

Lawson watched Merilee sleep, pulling the blanket more tightly around the two of them as they lay on the beat-up sofa. He couldn't believe he wasn't as exhausted as she. Their game had gotten pretty intense, and he'd made her come five times before bringing her inside and making love to her until she couldn't keep her eyes open. But he was wide awake.

Something was off. He could feel it. And he wasn't so sure he bought her excuse of being upset about her father. He knew she missed him desperately. But the pain that had flashed in her eyes was too raw, too unexpected. Too fresh.

No matter how much he racked his brain, he couldn't put his finger on an explanation. A part of him wanted to turn cartwheels at the thought she was upset he was no longer going to be part of her family business. That it was important to her for him to stay on. But there was no reason. John was ready enough, Lawson wouldn't be leaving otherwise, and Merilee was only a silent partner. Her life, what she loved, was elsewhere. She'd chased her dream and caught it. And now he was doing the same.

The clients he'd acquired for Diego Charters over the years would more than make up for any loss they'd see from some of his loyal clients following him. This fact allowed him to sleep at night. He studied Merilee's face as she slept. She looked peaceful, a departure from her drawn features earlier.

Did she want more from him? Had this diversion affected her as much as it had him? Did she want *him*, plain and simple? He traced the soft features of her face with his gaze. He could see that, he had to admit. Two days ago he would have passed out from laughing if someone had suggested Merilee Diego would somehow worm her way into his heart. But now…

Now it wasn't so funny. She hid a lot under the surface. And he liked every morsel he uncovered. Except the sadness. That he didn't like. But perhaps there was something he could do about it. His life was all about taking chances lately. Starting his own company, breaking ties with Diego Charters. And now Merilee.

She curled into his embrace, nuzzling his neck in her sleep. Yes. She was a chance worth taking.

* * * * *

Merilee checked her seat belt while Lawson finished his preflight check. It was secure. Same as five minutes ago when she checked the last time.

Being enclosed in such a small space with Lawson would be her undoing. He was all rainbows and unicorns this morning. He was probably thrilled to finally put all this behind him. Move on with his new life and kiss his past goodbye. He had affection for her—very carnal affection—of that she had no doubt. But their fling was over now and she had to somehow pick up the pieces of her life. Her boss at the school had been none too pleased when she'd put in for her leave of absence. She was on borrowed time there, and it wouldn't surprise her in the least if someone else had been put in her position by the time she finally made it back to New York.

Perhaps she'd just stay in Treasure Cay forever. That option was looking more appealing with each minute that passed. She could take her inheritance and buy a little house on the beach. Wear her hair in cornrows and—

"You all set?"

Lawson drew her back from what was becoming a

very plausible escape route fantasy. She could practically hear the shells clinking together as she swung her head to and fro.

She adjusted her mic so it was positioned in front of her mouth. "Yes. Of course. Let's do this."

"Try to relax during takeoff. Short runways can make those a little scary too. You might not want to look down until we gain some altitude."

She nodded. Knowing full well she'd look. Nothing could scare her more than what lay ahead in her life.

The Cessna sped down the limited runway and before she knew it they were airborne. And very close to the ocean. He wasn't lying. Not a reassuring view, by any stretch of the imagination. And she could actually see the sharks in the shallows. But soon they had enough lift that her instincts no longer told her she should fear a plummet to a watery death. Again.

Merilee could feel Lawson's regard on her, but she didn't have the heart to look his way. She didn't know what to think of his mood and kept looping back around to the most obvious reason. His new life was beginning. Who wouldn't be excited by that? If things had gone her way, she'd look as if she had a coat hanger in her mouth, her smile would be so big.

She'd woken in the middle of the night and watched Lawson sleep. It was then that she knew, without a doubt, that she loved him. Hell, she probably always had, since the first time she'd laid eyes on him when she was an impressionable teenager. Her dad had loved him, so she had always known on some level there was a very good reason why. Now she knew. He was kind, loyal, and put his own needs on hold until he was assured the show could go on without him. She wouldn't be the one to tell him that wasn't actually the case. He deserved his dream. And she knew, deep down, that her father would want this for him.

And in order for him to have it, he couldn't find out what was going on until it was too late for him to step in. He'd stay on and help her. No doubt about it. Even if that wasn't what he wanted. She slammed her eyes shut and fought back tears. And that meant she couldn't be around him. If he was part of her life, he'd know.

She knew what she had to do. She'd step off this plane and into her fake vacation at Treasure Cay, leaving Lawson, and her heart, behind.

"You're quiet," he drawled through the headset.

She pasted on a smile more fake than her brother's supposed support of her happiness and looked at Lawson. "You wore me out last night. Who knew palm fronds could be used in such a manner?"

"Well, it was definitely more imaginative than spelling out 'help' on the runway. And since there was a shortage of feathers, I had to find some option to tickle you with."

"You're definitely a good man to have around in a

pinch."

"I'm just getting started, darlin'." He winked at her and her heart sank. The look he gave her suggested more. More time together. More hot sex. More…everything. Prior to his confession by the fire, "more" was a word she could have gladly jumped onboard with. Now it was just something else she had to lose.

"Ah, how long until we touch down?"

He glanced at his watch. "Probably about another forty minutes or so. Why so anxious, got a hot date?"

He smiled, but it didn't reach his eyes, and she realized they'd never truly cleared that up. "No. Of course not. I just really need some time to myself now. I've got a lot going on, personally…with work, and I didn't want to admit I was going away by myself for mental health reasons. I thought you'd give me a hard time about it."

He reached for her hand. "I probably would have, being an ass and all."

She gave a genuine smile then. Damn, she was going to miss this man. "No doubt. But really, I've just rented a villa for a few nights so I can screw my head on straight. And what better place than a sunny island where everything seems brighter?"

"So you're back when?"

She was thinking so fast on her feet she was going to fall and bust her ass at any moment. She pulled a date from thin air. "Next Tuesday."

"Who's bringing you back?"

Crap. Something he could verify if he chose. "Damien. He's dropping off a family for some sort of reunion thing and I'm hitching a ride back."

"Damien…he's a good guy."

Good God. Please let that be the end of the inquisition.

"And what time—"

"Would you look at that," Merilee exclaimed, pointing out the window at a large yacht below. "Do you think it belongs to a celebrity?"

He craned his neck to get a look out her window. "Wow, that's a huge one. Could possibly be. Definitely someone better off financially than the two of us." He laughed and she let out a sigh of relief when he abandoned his line of questioning.

* * * * *

Lawson held his hand out and helped Merilee from the plane. "Here you are. Safe and sound at your destination." He placed a kiss on the inside of her wrist and could swear he felt her stiffen beneath the touch. He sent her a questioning look.

She gave him a weak smile and pulled her hand back, threading her fingers together in front of her. "Thank you, Lawson. This has been quite an…adventure. I don't think anyone could have handled it better than you."

Nodding, he studied her face. Something was way the fuck off. He supposed Merilee could be somewhat embarrassed about the purpose of the trip, but considering he'd had his face buried between her legs for a good portion of their time on the island, she shouldn't be this shy. "Well, let's get your bag. Do you have transportation lined up yet?"

She followed him as he rounded the plane to the baggage compartment. "Not yet, but there will be lots of locals outside the terminal who have taxis. Shouldn't be an issue."

Lawson unlocked the compartment and retrieved her bag and small carry-on. "Let's get these inside."

"Oh, I can get them," she said as she halted him with her arm.

Come again?

He'd seen Merilee in many moods over the years he'd known her, but this one he couldn't pinpoint. She wouldn't meet his eyes and her posture was stiff as a board. She seemed more and more like the woman he thought she'd been as each second passed. Could this entire thing have been some fling to her? Some way to escape the boredom of her fancy life up in New York? Certainly not…

"Let me at least walk you in, for crying out loud."

His tone struck home, for she did meet his eyes then. The warmth he'd relished over the last two days was gone, and the best way he could describe what he saw was impassive. She smiled at him, a smile one would bestow upon a passing stranger on the street, and said, "Of course. Thank you."

She walked ahead of him, head high, arms crossed over her chest. The princess was clearly back. With a huff, he yanked her suitcase into motion and repositioned her carry-on over his shoulder. She had a few yards on him and was already in the terminal by the time he caught up with her.

She pulled the bag from his shoulder and positioned it on top of her rolling suitcase. She placed her hand on his shoulder and gave him a beaming smile. "Again, Lawson. Thank you so much. For getting me here safely, for protecting the reputation of Diego Charters and for helping John so much. My father would be grateful." She leaned in and pressed a kiss to his cheek. "I wish you the best of luck in your new endeavor."

Lawson narrowed his eyes, but said nothing. No words came to mind that didn't start with, *What the fuck are you thinking?*

"If you're ever in New York," Merilee fiddled with the leather strap of her bag, "look me up. John has my address."

He snorted. "That's it?"

A delicate blush crossed her cheeks, but he couldn't tell if it was embarrassment or anger. When she met his gaze, he got his answer.

"What do you want me to say, Lawson? I know I'm not the first woman you've had a sex fest with, and if it were a different situation it never would have happened. You don't go after princesses, after all." She looked him dead in the eye. "Circumstances created the perfect situation for us to blow off some sexual steam and disregard how we really feel about each other."

"You're serious?" He placed one hand on his hip, rubbing his chin with the other. "That's what you thought that was?"

"You forget I've known you for a long time, and I know the way you operate. Let's not make this into some sort of drama. You've got things to do and so do I. As hot as the last two days were, that's just not reality. A classroom full of children is my reality. And you have a business to run."

White-hot fury burned up his spine and Lawson called on every ounce of patience he had to keep the reaction from her. He should learn to stick to his gut instincts. For years he'd thought her a selfish, self-involved *fucking* princess. And he was right. Well, screw her.

He bowed at the waist, in a manner that screamed sarcasm. "Miss Diego, it's been a pleasure. If you ever have need of a charter in the future…" He reached into his wallet and pulled out a business card. "Be sure to call your brother."

With that, he turned and left her in the terminal. He didn't look back. Mistakes were best left behind, and the last thing he wanted was to see the woman he'd mistakenly thought he might be able to give his heart to.

Merilee watched Lawson walk away and called upon all the strength she had not to break out in sobs and run after him. She'd had no idea how deeply his feelings ran. And they did run deep. There was no way to disguise the pain in his eyes when she'd been so cold to him. But the truth would only hurt him more. And if he changed his life to help her, he'd just grow to hate her in the end.

No, she'd done the right thing. For him. As for her? Well, back to more of what she knew. Solitude and a sense of failure. What would her father think of her? She couldn't even go there. She'd done what she felt was the right thing to do and that was the end of it. Unclenching her fists, she looked down at the crumpled card in her hand. *Diego Charters, John Diego, Jr.*

She wasn't welcome in Lawson's life or his plane. Considering how she'd behaved, that sounded about right.

CHAPTER EIGHT

It had been nearly a week since he'd left the princess at the Treasure Cay airport. Or, more accurately, she had left him. He'd give just about anything to say he hadn't spared her a thought since. But that simply wasn't the case. He'd spared her a thought and then some. She was the last thing on his mind at night and the first thing upon waking. To make matters worse, she haunted him in his dreams. Not the woman he'd left at the airport. The vulnerable woman who had lain beneath him, whispering his name, making him forget all the reasons she wasn't right for him. Or he for her.

And being called into the office by dickwad extraordinaire wasn't exactly his idea of a good Tuesday morning. He had a couple sets of keys to return, but originally it had been agreed he could bring those in Friday when he picked up his final paycheck. But until then, he was officially still under the employ of the Diego siblings, so here he was.

He stepped into the cool air-conditioned building and greeted the receptionist before heading toward John's office. He saw Damien walking toward him.

Why was that odd? He searched his brain for the answer but before it came to him, he'd reached his former coworker in the hall.

"Pretty heavy shit, huh?" Damien asked and clapped Lawson on the shoulder.

"What are you talking about?" Lawson thrust his hand through his hair. *Damien. Damien.* Then it hit him. "Hey, what are you doing here?"

Damien smirked. "Well, we're all here. For a while at least. Who knows what will happen next?"

The cryptic response went in one ear and out the other because it had nothing to do with what Lawson was asking. "No, what are you doing here right *now*? You have a charter to Treasure Cay this morning."

"Don't know where you heard that, but all the planes are grounded for a couple of days while John irons everything out with Barango Charters."

What the hell? "So who's flying to Treasure Cay to bring Merilee back?"

"Are you okay, dude? Did they screw you somehow in this deal?"

It would be a miracle if any of Lawson's back molars were left after this conversation. "I don't know anything about a deal. What I *do* know is that you were supposed to

102

take a charter to Treasure this morning and bring Merilee back with you."

"Merilee was back days ago. She had to be here Friday to sign paperwork for the sale of the company. We all found out about it when Barango's bigwigs came barreling through the office as if they owned the place. Which, as of this afternoon, they do, I guess."

"Excuse me?" Sweat broke out across Lawson's upper lip.

Damien shook his head, a look of disgust on his face. "Of all the people John should have told, it was you. I'm not sure I want to stay on at a place like this, no matter how so-called 'great' these new owners are supposed to be. John's an ass, if you ask me."

Lawson could only nod as various scenarios ran through his head. Had John used him to increase profits further to snag a company like Barango, relying on Lawson's love and respect for John's father to keep him around as long as possible? Lawson had done exactly that, even if it was only to allow him to leave with no regrets. And what of Merilee? Had she been trying to seduce something out of him? Find out what his specific plans were to protect her family business from any competition?

He shook his head. No. She hadn't once asked for any financial or operational details about her father's company. Or press for details of his new one. She'd only asked him to make her come again and again.

But…

She *had* asked him, if he could do anything he wanted, work anywhere he wanted, what would he do? And then he'd told her…and she'd seemed to close in on herself emotionally.

Shit. Something was wrong. Very wrong. And he knew just the asswipe he had to see to get the answers he needed.

* * * * *

New York was a far cry from the islands, even if they were experiencing unseasonably warm temperatures for May. And those unseasonably warm temperatures had made it onto the subway this morning, apparently. It was her own fault, really, for missing her alarm and leaving late for work when most other commuters were making the same trek. But she'd been up crying a lot of the night. Just as she had every night for the last week. The ride home had been no better.

Signing those documents while her brother stood over her had been one of the hardest things she'd ever done. Right behind watching Lawson walk away from her in that humid airport terminal. The only thing that gave her peace of mind was knowing he'd be living his dream. Within a matter of days, everything would be a done deal. The legal documents should already be complete and the new owners would hopefully keep things as close to how they were as possible. And her evil brother would be out in California "living the dream", as he called it. Whatever the fuck that meant, she had no idea. But good riddance. She was no longer tied to him in any way.

And who knows? Perhaps in time she'd contact Lawson. Tell her side of the story. There could be a teensy-tinsy chance he wouldn't hate her for all she'd done.

After she'd flown out of Treasure, the fact Lawson could be furious he wasn't told the truth had hit her like a semi and left her in a heap of near hysteria. She'd only been doing what she'd thought he would want. But did she really know what he wanted? Did she really know anything?

Her track record answered that with a resounding no. But as she told the students she taught, one can only do the best one can and move on from there. Many of her students had much to be ashamed of, including skirmishes with the law. But she saw them rise above it time and time again. She could do the same.

After she gave Lawson time to calm down.

She was all for bettering herself and practicing what she preached. But she wasn't a complete moron. Going to Lawson with an "I'm sorry" and a fancy set of underthings would not be the wisest course of action right now. And neither was remembering the things he could do to her body.

* * * * *

She hadn't been at Grayson Manor. And boy, had he

eaten crow on that one.

He cringed even now, thinking about his snide comment about rich kids needing distractions too, just like Merilee. When he'd arrived at the school, he'd quickly learned it catered to underprivileged children, and after talking to a few of her coworkers, discovered they practically worked for a song. Strike another mark under "ass" on his tally sheet.

Her chatty friends had informed him she'd taken a sick day, but for safety reasons, they had said, they weren't comfortable giving him her address.

No matter.

When he'd had his nauseating conversation with John, he'd gotten all the information he needed. And a lot he didn't want to hear. John had been shocked Merilee hadn't pleaded for Lawson's help. That was why he'd insisted Lawson fly her. Said he'd own up to being an ass, but wanted to give his sister at least a shot at maintaining the company if she could get Lawson onboard. In the end, John said, it appeared Merilee was just her usual self-involved brat, only interested in her life in New York, not carrying on the family name. And the bastard gave Lawson the *nudge nudge, wink wink,* as if they were on the same page. They weren't even in the same fucking book as far as Lawson was concerned.

And any small amount of respect he may have harbored for John's hard work over the years disappeared completely when he learned the lengths John went to in order to keep his plans from everyone for as long as possible. The employees, his sister and Lawson as well. Despite the fact Lawson's blood, sweat and tears over the last few years had gotten Diego Charters to a level that would entice a company the size of Barango. He'd taken pride in finishing what John senior had started.

But what was done was done. Merilee had signed the papers and fled to New York. Diego Charters was in the capable hands of one of the largest charter companies in the country, and John was off wherever pussies such as himself went once they'd screwed over everyone close to them.

Lawson paused at the apartment building and glanced at the number over the door. 295. This was the place. And it had a secured entrance. So much for his element of surprise. He didn't want to give her even two minutes to come up with some story about why she'd kept all this from him. He let out a heavy sigh and pressed the button for her apartment.

"Yes?" Her voice crackled through the intercom.

Sweat beaded on his forehead at the very real possibility she'd send him packing. One deep breath and then he took the leap. "Um, Merilee? It's Lawson. We need to talk."

The silence that followed was like a noose around his neck. He leaned his head against the wall, clenching his fists at his sides.

A buzz sounded and he jumped, grabbing at the door

handle. His heart sped as Lawson pulled open the door and glanced around for an elevator. A walk-up. She was on the fourth floor. With determined steps, he made his way to her apartment and knocked on the door.

Merilee opened it, a wary look on her face. She nervously ran her hand over her hair, much of which had pulled loose from a ponytail. Dark circles marred the skin under her eyes, and she wore pajama bottoms with ducks all over them and a fitted tank top. She'd never looked more beautiful.

"L-Lawson. What in the hell are you doing here?"

"May I come in?"

She glanced over his shoulder into the hall, her bottom lip between her teeth. No doubt hoping for rescue from a neighbor. Her shoulders drooped and she stepped aside, allowing him entrance. He entered her tiny apartment and gave it a cursory look before turning to face her.

Shit on a stick. Not only was she not ready to see Lawson now, but she most definitely was not ready to see him when she looked like this. As what could be described as unkempt at the best, homeless drifter at worst. She hadn't bothered changing out of her PJs this morning. Her cat and various houseplants didn't seem to mind her attire of misery.

But Lawson? Yeah, she cared about him. Once again,

she was ill-prepared to be around the sexy pilot she couldn't stop thinking about.

She yanked the elastic from her hair and quickly reassembled her mass of waves into what she hoped was a presentable state. She crossed her arms to conceal her braless nature and did her best to project a "this ain't no thang" air about her. She was failing miserably, she was certain.

"Um, what are you doing here?"

Lawson motioned toward her couch. "May we sit?"

With no other reasonable recourse, she nodded and followed him, taking a seat as far away as the armrest allowed. What looked like a smirk started to form on his lips but he quickly schooled his features and settled his gaze on her face.

"So, I was over at Diego Charters last Tuesday to turn in some keys. It's funny, but I ran into Damien."

"Damien?" *Oh crap.*

"Yeah, and what's funnier is that he said he never had a charter to Treasure scheduled for that day. In fact," Lawson crossed his ankle over his knee and laced his fingers on top, "he said there were no charters at all because your lovely brother had up and sold the company."

Merilee could literally feel the blood draining from her face. She knew Lawson would discover everything that had transpired and her role in it, she just hadn't counted on a personal play-by-play from the man himself. On her couch. While he looked all delicious. She averted her gaze.

"I know I probably should have told you—"

"You think?" She dared a look at him and his lips were set in a thin line. She imagined "princess" had been on the tip of his tongue. She felt very royal right now. A royal pain in the ass for fucking everything up so much.

She rubbed her temples. "Lawson, I had every intention of telling you. Of seeing if you'd be willing to give me some guidance, some help..." She drew a deep breath. "If you'd stay on if I bought out John, knowing you'd be taking on all the responsibility since I clearly have no head for business. Or other things, apparently." Her gaze dropped to her lap and she wrung her hands together. Was this moment any better than it would have been if she'd found the courage to ask straightaway, instead of trying to manipulate the situation?

The sofa cushion dipped as Lawson moved nearer. He placed his hand over her fidgeting ones and gave a light squeeze. Her heartbeat soared, but she couldn't be sure if it was from fear or simply his touch. "And then when I mustered the courage to ask you how you saw your future going, you were so...so..." The backs of her eyes pricked with a warning of tears, but she refused them.

Lawson took her chin in his hand and turned her face toward him. "And then I told you my grand plans and how happy I was about them. How happy I knew your father would be."

Merilee nodded and cursed her weakness when a tear slipped through her defenses and tracked down her cheek. Lawson pulled her against him until she was in his lap, her head resting on his shoulder. "I couldn't do it, Lawson. Not after getting to know the real you and finding out how important it is to you to make it on your own, just like my father did. It wouldn't have been fair. And..." She took a shaky breath. "Deep down, I knew I'd be disappointing my father. He wouldn't want his business run at the cost of someone's happiness. Your happiness."

"You should have told me." Lawson rested his head on top of hers and gently stroked her back. It took all she had not to wrap herself around him and let him soothe all her pain away. The pain she'd brought on herself and deserved. "But everything happens for a reason. I believe that."

She brought her head up to look at him, wiping stray tears from her cheeks. "What do you mean?"

"Have you gotten your copies of the papers from the attorneys yet?"

She ran the dates through her head. She should have had them by now. "Um...no, actually."

"Well, there's a good reason for that."

She turned in his lap completely then, staring at him straight on. "What does that mean?"

"Well, after Damien informed me of all the crap your

brother had pulled, I got good and pissed. I can't remember feeling so used or being so angry." He pinched the bridge of his nose and slammed his eyes shut.

Merilee waited him out, resisting the urge to comfort, to kiss him, to throw him down on the couch and give her body what it was screaming for, disaster in the making or no.

When he finally opened his eyes and focused on her once again, a calm had overcome him. "I interrupted the meeting John was having with the new owners and the attorneys and requested some time to speak with my lawyer before any final documents were signed."

"What?" Her mouth gaped. "Did you get John to change his mind? To let me buy him out?"

Lawson laughed without humor. "This is your asshole of a brother, remember? With the smell of money directly in front of him, there was no chance in hell that was going to happen."

Merilee deflated. Any sense of hope in the dreadful mess she'd created being rectified was gone. "So, why bring in attorneys of your own? You held no shares in the company. What could you possibly retain?"

He grinned then. A smile so bright it nearly blinded her. "I was given partial use of the name Diego Charters."

Confusion wrapped around her. "But that doesn't make any sense. At all." She shook her head. "I mean, the parent company would need it, right? It's been around for a long time."

"But not as long as Barango Charters. And it's not nearly as big or profitable as they are. Not by a long shot. As much as I'd like to think we're the most well-known, we're not. They had plans to change the name from the get-go. And unfortunately, most of the employees also. It wasn't too difficult to get them to sign the name over to me."

Hope unfurled in her belly, starting as a slow simmer and then radiating through her body to her fingers and toes. "And my brother?"

Lawson sighed. "He didn't care. His name—and more importantly, your father's name—meant very little to him in the end. He was only looking for the payout."

She should have been appalled and shocked, but she wasn't. From what she'd learned of her brother recently, this behavior fit the bill. Bastard. "So your new charter business…it's called Diego Charters?"

"Well, I did risk life and limb on that desolate island to protect the name. I've got to get something out of it, right? But no, they wouldn't agree to the exact name." He raised an eyebrow. A tease, but she knew there was more. "And honestly, what better way to honor the memory of my mentor, the man who treated me as his own son, than to repeat his success story? Start with something small and make it one of the top charters in the country."

"You're serious." That was the best she could come up with. She was overcome with emotion—gratitude, shock, relief, love and fear. And those last two were zingers. She knew she loved him back on Walker's Cay. Knew it when she walked away from him, and relived it each sleepless night since then. But she was afraid. Lawson had mentioned her father. He was honoring his memory by living out his dream. He'd said nothing about where she belonged in all this. If she did at all.

"I've never been more certain about anything in my life, Merilee. This is what I'm supposed to do. Every fiber of my being is telling me so." He drew her closer, grinning ear-to-ear.

She eased out of his lap and wandered to the window. "I'm so happy for you. *So* happy." And she was. Really. She felt his presence behind her even before his hands rested on her waist.

"What are you thinking?" he asked, his thumbs grazing her hipbones.

She turned to face him. Partial truth time. "I'm thinking how grateful I am that my wildly bad sense of judgment ended up costing you nothing in the end. I'm thinking how proud my father would be of you." She reached for his hands and squeezed gently before guiding them to fall back at his sides. "And I'm thinking how lucky I am to have gotten to know the real you back on that shambles of an island. It's a memory I'll keep with me forever."

She turned back to the window. She'd left out the part about how she wanted to throw her arms around him and

114

beg him not to leave her. To have her school somehow magically transported to Atlanta so she could continue doing what she loved, with the people she loved doing it with. She wanted to tell him she wished that she, like he, could have everything she ever wanted, with no regrets to tarnish it. But that was fanciful. And she'd learned the hard way that fanciful does not work.

"But what about me?" His voice arrested her depressing train of thought. He placed his hand on her shoulder and turned her around. "Is it only the memories you're interested in?"

She cow-eyed him, blinking in confusion. What was he talking about? His business was in Atlanta, had to be in the South for Caribbean charters in unpressurized planes if he hoped to make a dime, and even though he had the legal right to her name, that's about as far as it went from what she could see. "What are you saying, Lawson?"

"Well..." He gripped her hips and edged her closer until only mere inches separated them. "It seems a pity to me that there's currently no one at my company with the last name Diego." He eyed her up and down. "And there definitely isn't anyone as sexy as you. I've seen the female employees at Barango." He mock shivered. "Not a pretty picture."

A corner of her lip quirked. "You want me to do some sort of promotional thing for you? Take a picture or two to validate the name and provide what you seem to believe is some sort of eye candy?"

"No." He moved closer, if that was even possible, until she could feel his breath against her lips.

"What do you want then?" she asked, cursing her trembling limbs.

"You."

She sucked in a breath, her heart beating so fast she was certain he could feel it within the limited distance between them. "B-but I'm here. And you're...there. And I thought you didn't like me."

He threw his head back in a laugh. "Oh I like you, darlin'. A whole hell of a lot. I thought I made that abundantly clear on Walker's." He pulled her flush against him and she felt just how much he did, in fact, like her.

"But my job is here. I can't just—"

"Of course not. I was just at that school of yours. I would no sooner ask you to leave a place you're so needed than rip my fingernails off one by one. Your place is here."

"And your place is in Atlanta. Chartering Caribbean vacations." Stating the obvious. *Brilliant, Merilee.*

Lawson placed his lips against hers, gently nudging with his tongue until she granted him access. She clung to his shoulders as he explored her mouth and fisted the back of her tank top, easing her even closer. His erection dug into her hip and she moaned into his mouth. When they finally pulled apart, panting, he sent her a saucy grin.

"I *do* own a plane, darlin'. And you have the summers

off.""

She so wanted to buy into all of this. Wanted Lawson forever. But a small part of her was still freaked out beyond belief that it would never work. He would get busier and busier with charters, and the times they'd see each other would get further and further apart. And then she would lose him again.

She sighed. "But you know how busy you'll be starting up a company. There are only so many flight hours to be logged in a week. And so many of the charters are on weekends. I just don't see—"

His kiss stopped her. Stopped her but good. Before she knew what was what, he'd backed her to the sofa and pulled her down to straddle his lap. Her tank top was halfway off when he paused. "Damien can handle any weekend charters when I'm here with you. I wasn't the only one with a master plan, apparently. Got himself a mighty nice Beechcraft Bonanza with a large inheritance his grandfather left him. Lucky bastard."

He reached into his jeans pocket and withdrew a folded piece of paper and handed it to her. "This is only a copy, but I wanted you to see it."

Her brows drew together as she unfolded the paper. It was a legal document stating that Damien Rogers owned forty-five percent of the company. Her eyes shot to his. "He's your partner?"

"One of them." He withdrew a paper from his other pocket and handed it over.

Merilee placed Damien's copy on the arm of the sofa and unfolded the second piece of paper. This one had *her* name and stated she had a ten-percent ownership in Diego Manning Charters.

She drew in a sharp breath and looked at Damien's contract again.

Yep, Diego Manning Charters.

That he'd done this without knowing how she truly felt spoke volumes. He had faith in her. In them.

Tears filled her eyes. "Lawson, I can't accept this. I've done nothing to grow the Diego Charters name, and I certainly know nothing about running a business. I'm a teacher, for crying out loud."

"A teacher I happen to love." Her heart took off like a shot at his words. "Damien and I agreed that since it was originally your family business, you should be a shareholder. *We* don't expect anything from you—financial or otherwise." He waggled his brows. "I, on the other hand, expect a lot from you." He finished what he started, ripping her tank top over her head.

She gasped as cool air struck her already hard nipples. "Oh yeah?"

"Yeah." He placed a trail of kisses along her neck, to just below her ear. "I expect full access to this gorgeous body anytime I want it." She groaned as he traced the shell of her ear with his tongue before moving across her cheek to her lips.

He drew back and looked into her eyes. His were more turbulent than the stormy sky in Walker's had been. "And I expect your heart. If I'm fortunate enough to deserve it."

She threw her arms around his neck and molded her body to his. "It's yours. I'm yours. You can have my name, my body *and* my love."

He repositioned them so she was beneath him on the sofa and gave her a wicked grin as he divested her of her pajama bottoms and panties. He placed hot, open-mouthed kisses down her neck and chest before he stopped to look up at her.

"I'd buckle up then, sweetheart, because with what I have planned for this luscious body of yours, you could be in for a rough landing."

The End

Thank you for reading **Charlie Sierra Tango**!

My husband, who is a private pilot, and I took many trips to Walker's Cay before the tragic hurricane hit, and I always knew I'd place two characters there to fall in love. I just didn't know that they'd bicker so much. ;-) I hope you enjoyed their love story (and fighting!) as much as I enjoyed writing it. If so, I would greatly appreciate your help in spreading the word, either to friends or by leaving a review or rating at your favorite online book retailer. I appreciate you taking the time to read my work, and hope I can entertain you again in the future.

Sincerely,

Kendall Grace

Southern Exposure

A quick trip to visit her hospitalized mother is lasting longer than Anna had expected. About twelve *weeks* longer. It's not that she isn't used to taking care of her mom—Anna took over that job when her father died—but it's a little stressful vying for partnership in her New York law firm from the nowhere town of Liberty, Alabama. Fortunately the neighbor, a hot Southern charmer, is willing to keep her occupied.

Since Trey breached her defenses, he and Anna have been getting to know each other, in every way possible, all the while doing their level best to be discreet in this tiny, old-fashioned town. The woman he's coming to know is a far cry from the uptight lawyer he first met. And he likes the new Anna. A lot.

As her feelings for Trey deepen, Anna is torn between duty and desire. What she wants versus what she thinks she needs. Returning to New York, reverting to the formidable attorney her father molded, is the responsible thing to do.

Too bad that's not the woman Trey fell in love with…

Chapter One

Anna Reed slumped against the wall by the front door of her mother's cottage in Liberty, Alabama, pushing soaked tendrils of hair from her forehead with a shaking hand. She watched as the taxi's taillights disappeared down the long drive and into the distance before searching blindly for the decorative pot where the house key was hidden. A flash of lightning crackled in the night sky and Anna jumped, clutching her chest and stumbling over what felt like a giant bag of potting soil. Her stiletto heel slipped between the boards of the front porch, snapping off when she tried to right herself.

She slipped the shoe off and groaned. As if her day hadn't been sucky enough.

An emergency phone call to her office had launched her into a journey requiring three airports, two flights and a midnight taxi ride into Nowheresville. And now this. Anna glared at the mutilated shoe in her hand, grabbed its mate and tossed both over the porch railing with a disgusted sigh. She continued to feel around for the planter in the pitch-black night until her fingers brushed its smooth surface and she was able to extract the key from beneath. She unlocked the door and fumbled for the wall switch. Sighing in relief, she flipped it.

Nothing.

"Well that's just great," she muttered. "No power."

She pushed the door closed with her hip and leaned against it, tears threatening to slip over her lashes. She shook her head, willing the negative emotions away. She was just tired—the panic that had seized her before learning her mother would make a complete recovery must have finally caught up with her, rendering her an emotionally fragile mess. Everything would seem different in the morning. She just needed some sleep before she went back to the hospital.

Anna locked the door and took tiny steps to avoid tripping on anything as she made her way to the tiny spare bedroom. She unbuttoned her wet blouse and skirt as she went, letting the soaked garments fall to the floor. A clap of thunder roared in the angry night and Anna cringed as she slid her hand down the wall, searching for the bedroom. Her fingers met air and she eased through the open doorway. Reaching in front of her, she felt for the foot of the bed and groped the edge until she was able to drop on top of the mattress in a heap of exhaustion. Releasing a long sigh, she turned onto her side.

"You must be Annabelle."

Anna's hip met the floor with a thwack, her head

bumping the wall as she tried to gain her footing. "Damn it!" She scrambled to her feet, her pulse rioting. "Who are—"

The beam of a flashlight illuminated the small room in faint light and she gasped at the stranger who stood on the other side of the bed wearing a smile and very little else.

She lurched forward and yanked her grandmother's handmade afghan from the bed, curtaining herself. Meeting his gaze, she squared her shoulders. "Obviously you know who I am. So who the hell are you?"

He chuckled and rounded the corner of the bed, approaching her. She took a step back, her effort to escape thwarted by the wall.

"Sorry," he said, his voice a low, lazy drawl. "I'm Trey Jacobs. I live next door." He extended his hand.

Anna eyed him for a long pause before tucking the corner of the afghan under her arm and hesitantly accepting his gesture. "Anna Reed."

He narrowed his eyes slightly, tilting his head to the side. "Your mama calls you Annabelle."

"Yes, well," she pulled her hand from his warm, calloused grasp and wrapped her arms around her torso, "I prefer Anna."

"Alright." He moved toward her again and she took a clumsy step to the side and backed into the window, the blinds clattering against the glass. Anna heard a drawer in the bedside table slide open then the scraping sound of a match. A large pillar candle illuminated their corner of the room in a soft glow.

He turned to face her and she was met with her first full glimpse of Trey Jacobs. He stood before her in black boxer briefs, one hand resting lightly on his hip. His hair was mussed from sleep, sticking up in delicious disarray. It appeared to be a dark blonde in the limited light and she could just make out stubble on his square jaw. Anna's attention drifted to his chest, to the hard planes of muscle concealed beneath skin that looked as smooth and soft as suede.

He cleared his throat and her gaze darted back to his. Trey smiled liked the Cheshire cat, his eyes reflecting amusement. Anna snapped her mouth shut, which had apparently fallen open during her unabashed perusal of her mother's neighbor. "Um, the hospital staff said a neighbor had been with my mom. Was that you?"

He nodded and sat on the edge of the bed, gesturing for her to join him. She glanced at his wide expanse of skin and the brief stretch of black fabric before focusing her attention on the painting over his right shoulder. "Do you want to get dressed or something?" she asked.

His throaty laugh suffused her cheeks with heat. What in the hell was her problem? She was put under fire on a daily basis back home in New York. If it wasn't opposing counsel or a squirrely witness, it was her demanding boss hovering over her as she attempted to scrape and claw her way to a partnership. Trey was only a man. She looked down at him, at the corners of his eyes crinkled in amusement, his full lips, the way he ran long fingers into his hair to brush it from his forehead.

Yes, he was just a man. And the Grand Canyon was just a crack.

He placed his palms against his thighs as he leaned toward her. "My mama always said, 'If you ain't seen it before, you don't know what it is.'" He winked at her. "But I'll be glad to give *you* some privacy if you'd like to put on something more decent than that afghan."

Anna glanced down at the family heirloom she was clutching to her chest. The ice-blue lace of her bra and panties was visible through a multitude of holes that had stretched out over the years. Great. "I, ah, don't have anything with me. My suit is soaked and I didn't have time to go by my apartment before the flight here."

Trey stood and assessed her for a long moment, his eyes sweeping the length of her, pausing where her waist cut in above her hip and again at the swell of her breasts. Heat crept up her neck as he slowly raised his gaze to hers. "Why don't you borrow something from Ellen?" His voice was husky, the sound eliciting tingling in all kinds of intriguing places.

"Good idea. I'll just..." Anna pointed to the door beyond him and he stepped aside, gesturing for her to walk past. She prayed there wasn't an enormous hole across her ass as she scurried from the room and ran her fingers along the wall in the corridor until she found her mother's bedroom. Anna closed the door and leaned against it, letting the afghan fall to the floor. "Geez," she said on a sigh, rubbing her hand down her face.

The light in the adjoining bathroom flickered then came on. Wonderful. *Now* there was power. When she was stumbling around in her skivvies with a near-naked man waiting to greet her, no. But ensconced in the privacy of her mother's bedroom, completely free of hot, bed-disheveled men, let there be light. Anna flipped on the overhead fixture with a disgusted sigh and walked to the closet. She slid hangers down the rod. "What the hell?" she muttered. It looked like a country thrift store had exploded in the small space. Where were all the respectable clothes her mother had worn in New York? Her cashmere lounging pants, her expensive jeans, her Gucci, her Prada? What was all this crap?

Anna grumbled as she searched for something, anything she would consider putting on her body. Finally she located a black velour tracksuit and one lace-topped camisole to layer beneath it. Needing to give herself a good once over before going to solve the mystery of Trey Jacobs, she stepped into the bathroom and stopped short in front of the vanity.

Two eyes ringed in mascara stared back at her. The knot she had fastened at her nape that morning was now dangling over her shoulder, suspended by one stubborn lock of hair still clinging to the hairpin in a death grip. Her skin was fish-belly white, her lips void of even their natural pink hue. Overall, not a pretty picture.

Anna groaned, yanking the pin from her hair. She shook out its length, running her fingers through from scalp to ends. Her hair fell in thick waves around her face. A definite improvement. Next she borrowed some of her mother's facial cleanser and removed the offensive black smudges from around her eyes. Digging through the vanity drawer, she discovered an iridescent peach blush and a light coral lip gloss—not her usual color palette, but anything beat having the complexion of Wednesday from *The Addams Family*. A swish of mouthwash and Anna was as ready as she figured one could be to face the odd situation in which she found herself.

Who the hell was Trey Jacobs and, more importantly, why was he so at home lounging around half-naked…in her bed?

* * * * *

Trey fished through the kitchen cabinet, looking for the herbal tea he had seen Ellen prepare on countless occasions. Brushing coffee filters aside, he found the box of Pomegranate Green Tea hidden behind them. He glanced at the label. Caffeine-free. Not that he would be getting any sleep after his conversation with Anna, that was for sure.

Ellen had said her daughter was beautiful, but the woman who had jumped from the bed in horror made that term seem pedestrian. Even travel-weary with makeup streaked down her cheeks, Anna was the sexiest woman

Trey had ever seen. And the afghan... He'd never be able to look at one of the musty relics again without remembering how her pale skin and bits of blue lace had been showcased through the holes in the worn throw.

The teakettle shrieked and Trey retrieved two mugs from the cabinet. He placed a tea bag in each and was just pouring the water when he heard her in the doorway. He turned toward the table, a hot tea in each hand, but stopped when he saw her.

She was wearing some of her mother's clothes, the waistband of the pants rolled over to stay in place. Her face was scrubbed clean of her old makeup, and now in the light he could see that her eyes were an intriguing shade of blue—almost gray in the center with a darker hue around the edge of the iris. And her hair...it was the stuff of fantasies. Long and thick in a shade of blonde he'd never seen. It fell around her face in loose waves, the ends brushing the curves of her breasts. He stiffened behind the fly of his jeans, his mouth dry.

"So." Anna tilted her chin up, crossing her arms over her chest. "Why is it exactly that you're here? In my mother's home?"

Trey walked to the table and placed the steaming mugs atop it. "Why don't we sit?" He pulled a chair out for her. She studied him for a long moment then closed the distance between them in three long, graceful strides and accepted the offered seat.

"Thank you," she said, scooting the chair toward the

table. He joined her on the other side.

"I'm sorry if I startled you. I wasn't sure when you'd make it down, and I was so tired when I got back from the hospital I didn't think to leave a note." He blew on the tea and tested the temperature with his lips before taking a sip. "Not that you'd have seen it in the blackout, anyway."

She leveled her eyes on his. "Thank you for being with her at the hospital. I'm glad she wasn't alone."

"When they called, I rushed right over. Scared the bejesus out of me." Trey shook his head. "Thank God she's going to be okay."

Anna stared at him, her eyes narrowing slightly. "So, the hospital called you? When she was admitted?"

He took a swallow of the tea. "No, the paramedics, actually. I'm her emergency contact. They must have gotten the number from her cell phone."

"Wait," she said, shaking her head as if she were trying to rattle something out of it. "They called you first? My mother has you…" Her lips compressed into a thin line and she leaned her forearms on the table, staring him down. "Just what in the hell is your relationship to my mother, Trey?"

Trey sputtered his tea as he swallowed at the implication. He imagined the look on her face was the very one Ellen had spoken of when describing what a brilliant trial attorney Anna was, how she could extract blood from any turnip of a witness. He'd certainly crack under the pressure if he were on the stand under this kind of regard. He bit the inside of his cheek, trying not to smile at her barely contained outrage.

"Anna," he said, mimicking her posture. "Your mother and my mother grew up together here in Liberty. My mom's family owned the house next door." Trey saw Anna's shoulders relax a fraction. "And like your mom, she moved away once she got married."

"Oh," Anna said, and brought the mug to her lips to take a sip. Placing the tea on the table, she eyed him expectantly.

"My mom died about five years ago and she left her parents' house to me. Eventually I got tired of the city, so I moved to Liberty. The house was a wreck, so I'm doing repairs around my other jobs. Plumbing's torn out right now, so Ellen told me I could sleep here until I finish it."

The corners of Anna's lips turned down. "I'm sorry about your mother. I lost my dad a little over two years ago, so I can relate."

"Thank you."

Anna nodded, clicking her fingernails against the mug. "So you're doing the work on the house yourself?"

"Yep. The addition to your mom's house as well. I'm a carpenter."

"Jacobs Construction," Anna murmured.

Trey had received the initial deposit for the necessary addition for Ellen's business, Belle's Buds, from Anna herself. As he watched her face, he could see it all coming

11

together.

She sat up in her chair, stretching her neck from side to side. "And how is it I've never met you, Trey?" Her voice dripped with suspicion, and he guessed he couldn't blame her.

"I've only been here six months. The city just got to me. I wanted something smaller."

"Where'd you move from?"

Trey leaned back and draped his arm across the chair next to his. "Birmingham."

The corners of her lips twitched. "Birmingham is the big city you escaped from?"

He smiled at her amusement. "What can I say? I like towns with one stoplight."

"They've put a stoplight in Liberty?" She arched an eyebrow.

"Sure did. Over by the Stop 'n' Shop. Old Mr. Wilkes plowed his Lincoln into a car turning into the parking lot a few months back, so I figure the town thought it was about time."

Anna snorted and covered her mouth with her hand. "Sorry. It's just, you know, coming from New York…"

Trey caught the sparkle in her eyes as she wrapped her head around what must seem absurd to a big-city girl. "But Liberty isn't a complete mystery to you. Ellen said you spent some time in the summers here as a kid, and you were here to help her start up her business."

"That's true." Anna glanced around the kitchen. "And Lord knows Mom did her best to infuse an air of Alabama up in New York, making sure her Southern roots took hold and grew strong in our home. But the town of Liberty has always seemed so foreign to me. So different from what I'm accustomed to."

"I would guess so." Trey studied her as she drank her tea. There was a sophisticated presence about her that he hadn't seen in a woman in a long time. Even having been drowned in the rain and forced to borrow clothing two sizes too big, she exuded class and refinement. She would stand out in Liberty like a Union soldier on the Confederate's frontline.

Anna rubbed her temple, her eyes drifting closed, and Trey was brought out of his armchair analysis of the city mouse thrust into the country. He rose from the table and circled around to her chair. "Come on, you're exhausted. Why don't you go to your mom's room and get some sleep? I'll drive you to the hospital in the morning."

"Okay. Thank you," she said softly as she rose. She picked up her mug and walked to the sink, where she deposited it in the white ceramic basin. When she leaned against the edge of the counter and lowered her head, Trey approached, placing his hand on her shoulder. She tensed beneath his touch.

"Are you okay, Anna?"

She nodded and angled her body away from him. He heard a muffled sniffle. If there was one thing he couldn't bear, it was a woman in tears. Blame it on his upbringing, his mother, whatever, but he didn't have it in him to just let it be—whether it was any of his business or not. And Anna didn't strike him as a wilting flower. Hell, she could probably annihilate most men's attempts to get near her with a practiced raise of her eyebrow and a piercing look from those incredible eyes of hers. But none of that stopped him from touching her again, placing his hand on her wrist and turning her to face him.

Her eyes were brimming with tears she attempted to blink away. One spilled over and Trey brushed it from her cheek with his thumb. "It's okay to be upset, Anna. You've been through a lot today."

She jerked her head back from his touch, confusion mixing with the tears in her eyes, but she didn't step away from him. Trey breathed in her scent. She smelled of rain and some sort of wicked perfume meant to bring men to their knees. A scent so enticing a man could only step closer to consume it. So he did.

Anna's eyes grew wide as he moved but she stood as still as lake waters at sunrise, tilting her head to look up at him. He knew he was going to kiss her. No matter how inappropriate it may be, he hadn't a choice. Not when her eyes met his, her breath hitching when he cupped her cheek in his hand, her lips parting on a sigh as he slowly lowered his head.

He had meant for his kiss to be tender, to comfort her, but as soon as his lips met hers, everything changed.

She wound her arms around his neck and pulled him into the kiss, deeper and deeper, until they were both clinging to one another with greed—hungry mouths and tongues and hands. Trey groaned as she stepped into him, running his hands into her hair to anchor her mouth against his. Anna's fingers found the edge of his t-shirt and she burrowed underneath, splaying her palms against his chest as she drew his tongue into her mouth.

Jesus.

Trey backed her into the counter and pressed kisses against her jaw, his hand sliding up her rib cage. As he neared her breast, she whimpered, the tips of her fingers digging into his flesh. He closed his palm over a round globe, his mouth seeking hers once more. She pressed her body closer, trailing the tips of her fingers down his abdomen.

Trey hissed in a breath and slid his hands around to her ass, pulling her flush against his erection. Anna stilled beneath his touch before she tore her mouth from his, turning her head to the side. Stunned, Trey took a step back.

"I-I can't believe I just did that," she said and placed the back of her hand against her lips. "I don't know what came over me. I must be out of my head with fatigue." She wrapped her arms around her torso protectively and turned away from him.

"Anna." He tried to touch her arm but she stepped out of reach.

She swiveled slowly on her heel to face him. Her lips were still swollen from his kisses and her hair was sexy wild. He became even harder, if that was possible. He started toward her but she shook her head and eased back another step.

"This was a mistake. I should go to bed," she said as she gathered her hair in her fist at her nape. "It's been a long day."

Trey drove his hands into his pockets, to hide his erection if nothing else, and nodded. "Alright."

Her cheeks flushed a soft pink. "Well, okay then. Goodnight." She waved at him awkwardly and turned to leave.

"Hey, Anna?"

She pivoted slowly to face him. "Yes?"

"Sweet dreams."

He smiled as he watched her nod and scoot out of the room. He knew his dreams would be filled with what it would be like to feel her writhing body beneath his, the look of desire she'd have in her eyes as he slid inside her, and the soft cries she would make when he brought her to completion. That is, if he could fall asleep at all.

She'd called it a mistake. Well, if that was the case, he hoped he'd get the opportunity to screw up again. Really, really soon.

* * * * *

The sun was just beginning to filter through the thick line of oaks surrounding her mother's property when Anna stepped into the new addition of the tiny cottage. Floor-to-ceiling windows lined the perimeter of the room, showcasing her mother's gardens. A refrigerated room jutted off to the right, two large glass doors with stainless steel handles the entrance point. The hum of the cooling system vibrated from just outside one of the windows. Anna peered inside at the empty shelves, shelves that would soon be filled to overflowing with wedding flower orders and floral arrangements to be delivered to the local stores and markets.

Belle's Buds had really begun to take off, allowing her mother to utilize her talent and passion for gardening. The growth made this addition a necessity, an expense added to Anna's already full financial plate. Her mother had protested, of course, but it was what it was. Their choices had been to move forward or stand still. And standing still wouldn't bring in any income or get her mother closer to realizing her dream of a sprawling, successful nursery. With her father gone, Anna took on the financial burden. It was her mother, after all, a woman who had devoted her life to her husband and daughter. It was Anna's turn now.

She wandered to the corner of the room where an office had been constructed, including a built-in desk and shelving system. Anna ran her hands along the curved detail of the desktop, kneeling to study an intricate floral pattern etched into the farmhouse-style legs supporting the weight of the workspace. She traced the bloom of a rose with the tip of her finger, following its wooden stem to the base that was carved into a leaf pattern. Anna had never seen anything like it.

Not unlike the man who had constructed it. Anna slammed her eyes shut as she replayed the scene in the kitchen for the hundredth time. It had flickered through her head in slow motion all through the night, reducing her to fitful tossing and turning. In the light of day, her behavior wasn't any more bearable. She had climbed on Trey like a kitten just coming into its claws. She had been desperate. Needy. And okay, turned on beyond belief.

Anna couldn't even remember the last time she'd had sex. Sure, she dated, if you called suffering through countless dinners with men who perceived themselves so witty and such good catches that they really needn't put in time to discover anything about *her* dating. There wasn't a one in the lot she could even imagine allowing to touch her. Much less in the way she had offered herself up last night, like some kind of tart on a free-for-all. And in the wake of her mother's accident, no less. The stress she'd been under must have obliterated the portion of her brain in charge of keeping her from making a complete ass of herself.

Anna placed her hand on the desktop and rose. The hairs on the back of her neck stood as well at the sound of boots scuffing across the temporary plywood flooring. Prickly heat crept up her neck like a climbing vine,

18

bursting into full bloom across her cheeks. Her fingers dug into the desk when Trey stopped directly behind her.

"Good morning," he said, his voice lending itself to that soft, smoky quality only a true Southern-bred man could employ. The kind of timbre a woman could cozy up to in inalterable bliss and listen to all day long.

Anna cleared her throat and turned to face him. "Good morning." Her breath stilled in her lungs at the look she saw in his eyes. Their piercing blue depths held her rooted to the spot, his intent stare letting her know in no uncertain terms he had relived their encounter a time or two as well and, when his gaze dropped to her lips, that he would like to again. Anna swallowed, focusing on his mouth. Desire pulled taut inside her, her pulse dancing in long-forgotten, passion-induced anticipation.

Remembering her mother, her entire reason for being in this little town of nowhere, Anna stepped to the side, averting her gaze.

Plastering a smile to her face, she looked back at him and pointed to the desk. "This is really something, Trey. The craftsmanship is just beautiful."

Trey leaned his palm on the smooth wood surface. He studied her for a long moment, making a slow sweep of her body before he raised his gaze to hers. "Thanks. Ellen and I found the legs for the desk at a flea market. The original table was scratched all to hell and missing one leg. Guy practically paid us to haul it away."

"Amazing," Anna murmured. "I'm very impressed."

He shrugged, a slow smile crossing his features.

Anna glanced around the room as silence ensued, purposely avoiding looking at Trey. She felt his regard on her, and when she dared a look, found the same intent expression in his eyes that threatened to incinerate her underwear. The same pair she'd been wearing since yesterday. A rather unpleasant circumstance she needed to remedy as soon as she left the hospital. His attention dropped to her mouth once more and she realized her underwear wasn't the only thing she needed to remedy.

"About last night, Trey..."

He took a step toward her, resting his hand on her hip gently. "Um-hmm..." His fingertips pressed into her, easing her toward him.

He smelled spicy and warm and reckless. Anna swallowed down the contented sigh she felt gurgling to life in her chest. Wrapping her fingers around his wrist, she did her best to ignore the rapid fluttering of his pulse and stepped back. "Um, Trey. The way I behaved last night... I don't usually do that sort of thing." One corner of his lips quirked up. Damn him. "I mean, with men I hardly know."

Anna didn't like feeling like this. So out of control...so flustered...so unsure of where to go next. It was an emotion she wasn't accustomed to dealing with and she felt as out of place as a socialite at a monster truck jam. She drew in a deep breath. "And I just think it would be better if we forget what happened last night." She furrowed her brow. "Well, not forget, because it was nice, but, maybe it's best..."

His gorgeous lips transformed into a full-on smile, the corners of his eyes crinkling.

Good Lord Almighty. She was speeding off-course like a derailed train and if she didn't get control and put on the brakes soon, she would explode in a spectacular burst of humiliation.

"What I mean, Trey..." Anna cleared her throat. He took a small step toward her and she began a mental scramble for straws, deciding to pretend he was the opposing counsel's witness. Trey reached out and ran the backs of his fingers down her cheek.

Okay. Mock trial's off. "Here's the thing. I find you very attractive. Clearly."

"Clearly," he echoed, his attention zeroing in on her mouth for the third time. Her girly bits stood up and cheered in a consuming rush of heat that demanded attention. She tried to ignore them.

"But I'm only here for a few days and I'm not the kind of woman who gives in to this sort of...distraction." She was the type of woman who needed, desperately, to give in to exactly what he had on the menu. It was just the check full of complications she didn't know if she'd be willing to pay afterward.

He eased even closer and slowly pushed his hands into his front jeans pockets. He studied her for a pregnant pause before he leaned forward, stopping mere inches from her face. She sucked in a breath. "And just what kind of distraction is it, Annabelle?"

Her birth name flowed from his lips like gooey honey, rendering her insides to the same consistency. She knew just what kind of distraction he was—the kind that obliterates your mind and hijacks your thoughts. The kind an attorney fighting for partnership didn't have time to entertain, no matter how scrumptious it may be. "It's an, um, unwanted distraction."

A smile bordering on cocky graced his face. "My apologies, Anna. I certainly don't want to distract you from, well, whatever you're focused on."

She eyed him speculatively but he only smiled and waited her out. "Okay," she said, forcing a breezy air about her. Hot air was all she was filled with, but whatever moved her through the awkwardness would have to do. "So we're good?"

Trey leaned a hip on the desktop. "Right as rain, I'd say."

"Excellent." Anna rubbed her palms together before extending her hand. "Friends?"

He took her hand and brought it to his lips. "Why not?" he murmured and her traitorous heart turned cartwheels from the touch. "Can't have too many friends, right?"

She tugged her hand from his grip and nodded. "That's right." Anna glanced around the room, uncertain what to do with her new *friend*. "Hey, Trey," she said finally, taking what she hoped was a subtle step back. "Do you think you could take me to a car rental agency after the hospital? I'm going to need some form of transportation if I'm going to be here for a few days."

"Hmmm…" He looked at the ceiling, rocking back on his heels.

"If it's too much trouble, I can just call a cab or something," she offered.

He grinned at her, twin dimples winking from his cheeks. "No, it's no problem. I'm just trying to figure out where to take you. The nearest agency is probably a good drive into Huntsville, but there's Everett's here in town. If we're lucky, he'll have one in to rent."

"Um, okay." Anything that would take her to underwear and clothing and out of the mercy of his transportation was just fine with her.

Trey glanced at his watch. "It's about that time. Nurse said to come back around eight. You all set?"

"Sure," Anna replied. "Let's go."

Other Available Books by Kendall Grace

Southern Exposure

A quick trip to visit her hospitalized mother is lasting longer than Anna had expected. About twelve *weeks* longer. It's not that she isn't used to taking care of her mom—Anna took over that job when her father died—but it's a little stressful vying for partnership in her New York law firm from the nowhere town of Liberty, Alabama. Fortunately the neighbor, a hot Southern charmer, is willing to keep her occupied.

Since Trey breached her defenses, he and Anna have been getting to know each other, in every way possible, all the while doing their level best to be discreet in this tiny, old-fashioned town. The woman he's coming to know is a far cry from the uptight lawyer he first met. And he likes the new Anna. A lot.

As her feelings for Trey deepen, Anna is torn between duty and desire. What she wants versus what she thinks she needs. Returning to New York, reverting to the formidable attorney her father molded, is the responsible thing to do.

Too bad that's not the woman Trey fell in love with…

Northern Exposure

Roslyn can't get to the nowhere town of Liberty, Alabama, where her good friend Anna lives fast enough. She screwed up big time at her law firm in New York. Disappearing in the Deep South seems like the perfect solution to clear her head and figure out where to go from here. A hot roll in the hay with a smoldering fellow out-of-towner is a welcome distraction. How was she to know he was the local preacher's son? Oops.

Wren has one objective—land the contract that will put him on the map as a business broker. So what if he has to kiss ass and portray himself as the perfect preacher's son to earn the trust of the business owner. He's survived worst in his past. But the temptress who seduces him is exactly who he doesn't need to be seen with if he wants to pull off this charade. Too bad he can't resist her.

Thunderstruck

Desperate to distance herself from her previous life, and her high-powered ex, Jo Montgomery moves to a tiny slice of Georgia, an impetuous decision if ever there was one. Though not nearly as impetuous as throwing herself into an intimate relationship with her new neighbor. Hawk Stephens, a horse breeder and local celebrity, is sex personified, a man built for dark deeds in dark places. But he wants far more from Jo.

Every instinct tells Silent Hawk that Jo is The One,

and despite her obvious uncertainty, his Apache beliefs give him faith. The signs are unmistakable. His skittish little filly requires a strong hand, patience…and blazing, mind-bending sex that leaves no doubt to his feelings and intentions.

But before their love affair has barely begun, the reemergence of Jo's ex, coupled with a potentially tragic event, forces Jo to make decisions that not only damage Hawk's beliefs, but could also shatter their tender romance beyond repair.

Coming Soon

Innocent Exposure
Book Three in the Southern Heat Series

Abigail Dawson was always the perfect preacher's daughter. Pure of heart, body and soul. Until Johnny Williams broke her heart into a million pieces and she retaliated in the most stupid way possible. A mistake she can never take back—or face. Her only saving grace is that no one ever found out.

Johnny screwed up, big time, and lost the woman he loves in the process. Resigned to do anything to get her back, he puts himself front and center in her life. Not difficult to do in the tiny town of Liberty, Alabama. But just when he thinks he's making headway, she pulls back. Way back.

With time Abigail starts to forgive herself—and Johnny—and can see a future between them. But just as she's about to open her heart to him again, her mistake comes back to haunt her. With no place to hide in this little slice of the South, Abigail must own up to her transgression. Or walk away from Johnny forever.

Come Undone

New Adult

My sister became dependent on painkillers after a skiing accident left her leg broken in three places. I didn't understand and, yes, I judged her. After all, we were talking about her will. No one was forcing those pills down her throat. It seemed very cut-and-dried to me back then. But I know differently now.

The first time Stone touched her, Jane finally understood addiction…understood the aching need, the keen want for more…more of his hands…his mouth…his tongue. His complete mastery over her body. She knew the suffocation of crushing anxiety as she waited for her next hit, the flash of terrific pain when it didn't come.

Stone seems unwilling to give Jane what she needs; what she ultimately craves above all else. But addicts can't think beyond the fix. They'll resort to desperate measures to feed their need…even if they lose themselves in the process. Even if they come undone…

Playing for Keeps

New Adult

Pasts are best left behind, hidden deep in your memory—that is where I buried mine. The feel of his hands and mouth on my body, the way I lost myself in his touch. I fought so hard to forget. But just the sight of Christian brought it all back, forcing me to become consumed by him. Again.

Years before I had watched him, craved him—a guitarist in a band riding the wave to stardom—my brother's best friend. On the verge of womanhood, I never dared to reveal how I yearned. Until a cold New Year's Eve when I offered myself as the woman I'd become, bringing to fruition all I'd desired. As that night turned, so did my life. Devastatingly so. I never dreamed I'd become another of his one-night stands.

Can pasts can be exorcised if they come back to haunt you? And when a notorious playboy who broke your heart offers you his...how do you know if he's playing for keeps?

About the Author

Kendall Grace grew up in the Deep South, where she was taught to be all things Southern and proper. She always had a love for reading, but her passion for racy romance blossomed when she snuck a copy of *Forever* by Judy Blume past her mother at the bookstore. She's never strayed from that path.

She now resides in a large city in the South with her husband and two kids. When not performing the tasks of a Domestic Goddess and working the day job, she loves to sit down and write about steamy Southern men and the women who get caught up in their sexy drawls and chivalrous ways. She loves to hear from readers, so please visit her at www.authorkendallgrace.com

Visit Kendall's website for a complete booklist and other information:

www.authorkendallgrace.com

Email Kendall:
kendall@authorkendallgrace.com

www.ingramcontent.com/pod-product-compliance
Lightning Source LLC
Chambersburg PA
CBHW071625140626
46555CB00021B/382